THE WORLD IN GRANDFATHER'S HANDS

THE WORLD IN GRANDFATHER'S HANDS

by Craig Kee Strete

Clarion Books ✤ New York

Clarion Books
a Houghton Mifflin Company imprint
215 Park Avenue South, New York, NY 10003
Text copyright © 1995 by Craig Kee Strete

Type is 12/15-point Garamond

Printed in the USA

Library of Congress Cataloging-in-Publication Data
Strete, Craig.
    The world in Grandfather's hands / by Craig Kee Strete.
        p.   cm.
    Summary: Eleven-year-old Jimmy is upset when he and
his mother must move from the pueblo to the city after his father's
death, but his grandfather's patient philosophy of life helps Jimmy
slowly adjust.
    ISBN 0-395-72102-4
    1. Indians of North America—Southwest, New—Juvenile
fiction. [1. Indians of North America—Southwest, New—Fiction.
2. Grandfathers—Fiction. 3. Death—Fiction.] I. Title.
PZ7.S9164Wo   1996
[Fic]—dc20
                                  94-26799
                                  CIP
                                  AC

BP   10 9 8 7 6 5 4 3 2 1

For two in love with words
and for whom I have a love bigger than words,
Arnold Adoff and Virginia Hamilton.

THE WORLD IN GRANDFATHER'S HANDS

Chapter ⚡ One

I tried to put some of my father's things in the car. I did it quietly when I thought nobody was looking, taking them from the pile we were supposed to leave behind.

I had his fish-skinning knife with the wooden handle carved in the shape of a bear. I had the feather-tied wooden flute he used to play in the evening when the sun went down behind the walls of the pueblo.

My mother grabbed my arm while I was trying to open the car door.

"Jimmy, not those things," she said. "They belong here. We have no use for them in the city."

She seemed angry. I didn't know why she was so angry. It had been more than a year since Father died and she was still upset all the time.

"But I want something to remember him by," I said, trying not to look at her because I did not want to cry. I'm eleven and tall for my age, and I'm too old to cry.

"You have his eyes and his smile," Mother said. "And you carry him in your heart. That is enough."

"I won't leave these," I said and wrapped my arms around Father's things defiantly.

My mother gave me another angry look as if I had said something hateful. She acted so strange, these days. She didn't talk much anymore, and it had been that way ever since my father died. All these months and still her hurt was so great.

She started to move toward me. I thought she was going to just take the stuff away from me.

A shadow crossed my face and I looked up and saw Grandfather Whitefeather standing beside me. He motioned her away with one hand, and she turned and went back into our house to get more of our things.

"Jimmy, what are you afraid of?" asked Grandfather Whitefeather. He ran his hand down the length of his dusty old car, as if petting an old pony.

"I'm not afraid of anything. I just want some of his things. They belonged to my father and now they belong to me!"

Grandfather Whitefeather shook his head no. He seemed sad about the way I was acting.

"Things are meant to be used," he said. "Think of the sweet music that will go from this pueblo when this flute is gone. It will sit silently in a box on your shelf, and every day that it is not played, some of its beauty will die."

Grandfather held his hand out to take my father's things.

He smiled sadly. "Oh, you do not have to tell me what you are afraid of. You are afraid that you will forget him. But you will not."

"How do you know that?"

Grandfather looked back at the pueblo, at the houses of our people. His eyes seemed to stare through the walls and into the homes. I knew he was remembering. It was a little while before he spoke.

"Believe me, Jimmy, learning to forget, that is the hard part of life," said Grandfather.

He held his hands out to take the things from me, but I backed away from him so he would know I didn't mean to give them up easily.

"Come with me. Let your mother finish her packing and her goodbyes. Let us look at the land once more." Grandfather Whitefeather turned and began to walk away slowly with the bad limp he had.

I fell into step with him, and we walked out to the edge of the mesa and looked out over the land. It shimmered in the summer heat.

He looked up at the heavens. "The stars are up there in the sky, but you cannot see them now," he said. "Do you know the meaning of the stars?"

I shook my head no. I still had the knife and flute

clutched tightly in my hands. I didn't care what Mother or Grandfather said. I wasn't going to give them up.

"In the first days of the world, when the fathers of our fathers arrived in the house of the Great Spirit that is the sun, they saw four doors. One door for each of the sacred directions. Because life on Earth was hard, the Great Spirit opened each door with the wind, and said choose anything that you see."

I started to speak, but he motioned me to be quiet.

"You wonder how this is about your father and your mother and the loss you feel? Be patient." His hands came up and pointed slowly east, north, south, and west.

"The first three doors opened onto worlds of great wealth. A man who walked through those doors would be rich beyond the dreams of men. But our fathers' fathers did not go there."

The wind blew little eddies of dust around our feet, and Grandfather Whitefeather looked off to the west, shading his eyes against the sun.

"When the fourth door was opened, before them were the stars. The Great Spirit said, 'This is knowledge. I give it to you. But you must understand that knowledge has no end.' And that was the gift they chose."

I wasn't sure I knew exactly what he meant by that story.

"If you try to take your father's things with you,

you choose the wealth of the first three doors. That is not the way of our people. It is better to take the stars," he said.

"But my mother is just so angry. If she weren't so angry, I think she would let me take his things. I just don't understand why she's acting this way," I said.

"Your mother is brave and you must be brave like her. Perhaps she seeks to understand the stars. She is angry because what has happened cannot be changed. Your father took his name out of the world. Death comes for us all and no one can change this, as no man can change the stars," said Grandfather Whitefeather. "You must try to understand that my son and your father is gone from this world and he has taken his things with him."

"I'd still like to have something to remember him by," I said, and looked to the west to see what Grandfather was staring at. There was only the desert, stretching out as far as I could see.

"I know you do not understand. But your mother sees the stars in the night of your lives and does not want you to take any of your father's things with you. So respect her wishes."

"Does she hate him now?" I asked.

"No. She loves him more than ever," said Grandfather Whitefeather. "That is why it hurts her so much to have his things around reminding her of him. If she puts them away from her, she will remember him in a different way."

"It still doesn't make sense to me," I said. But I

thought about the way she cried at night now, and I gave in.

Grandfather Whitefeather took the knife and flute from my hands and put them in a thick leather pouch that hung from his belt. We sat there for a while, listening to the wind moving across the mesa. It was a chance to sit quietly for one last time, and I was glad to be able to do it. After a slow, silent time had passed between us, we walked back toward the house.

Grandfather took my father's things back inside and left them on the floor next to the small pile from which I'd taken them. Mostly it was just Father's clothes and his boots. That was just about all he had. My father always said we are not the kind of people who own things, because they end up owning you.

I stopped trying to understand it all. My father always said much of life is just lived and not understood. We do things because we have to do them. We don't always know why.

Maybe I would understand all this when I got older.

Maybe I would never understand. All I knew now was that I hurt inside, and nothing was going to stop that.

Chapter ⚬ Two

I was supposed to help Mother carry our stuff to the car, but there were already so many people helping her I felt more like a nuisance than anything.

Besides, it was mostly secondhand junk anyway. My father said houses should be filled with found objects. Sometimes when he was working near big cities, he and some of the other men from the pueblo would cruise around in their pickups on the nights when the white people put out their trash. They would come back with chairs and tables, old rugs, clothes, all kinds of stuff. We got some of our pots and pans that way. Of course, some of that junk was what my mother wanted to take along.

I didn't understand why we could take the junk and not the personal stuff that meant something to me. I just couldn't figure my mother out on this.

I remembered when a bus full of tourists came to the pueblo one summer. Usually we were too far away from the main road for tourists, but this was some kind of special tour. My mother was cleaning house that day, so she had put all our stuff outside. I was just sitting around, waiting for her to finish sweeping so I could drag everything back in.

A whole bunch of people got out and started taking pictures of me and of all our household stuff. One guy came up to me and said he was sorry we didn't have anything and that we were so poor, and he tried to give me money. I wanted to take the money because I figured he was probably drunk and would lose it somewhere anyway, but my father came along just then. He wouldn't let me take it.

Father was polite and thanked the man but told him we were not poor. He said we were rich, not in things, which don't count for much here in the pueblo, but in having each other.

Now that he was gone, we were poor again.

What we had mostly now were my mother's clothes and mine and some dishes and a few pots and pans. The biggest pile was the vegetables, corn, and squash from our own garden and from our friends' gardens.

My mother was busy with her friends from all over the pueblo who'd come out to help us make our escape.

I thought it was a rotten idea to leave. This pueblo was the only place I'd ever known.

I had to say goodbye to all my friends early this morning. My mother said I should get it over with, saying goodbye, because it would be a very long time before we came back this way again.

My grandfather Whitefeather lived in the city. He'd lived there since before I was born. It was his car we were loading our stuff into, a shiny, old Buick with one missing fender. His generation left the pueblo, many of them, when times were bad. My father was of the generation that came back here to live. I asked him why once, and he said it was for the same reason, that times were bad then, too. He said people often do different things for the same reason.

My grandfather worked in the city. Like my father, he used to work on highways and bridges. One day he was offered a chance to work in high steel in the city. He helped build some buildings that were more than twenty stories tall, and some twice that high.

It was dangerous work and my grandfather loved it. He said there was something great about working so high above the ground that the clouds got to know your name. Lots of Indians work in high steel.

But there was an accident one day and my grandfather got badly hurt. He was in and out of lots of hospitals for a long time. Finally they sent him home and said he was going to be all right, but he couldn't work high steel anymore. He got a small pension, which he used to pay for a house in the city.

He always hoped someday his legs would get

9

well enough for him to work in high steel again, but it never happened.

We visited the city once, but I was so young I didn't remember what it was like. Mother said she hoped I would like it. Grandfather said I wouldn't at first but might learn to later.

I hated it already and we hadn't even left.

I got in the car. It was pretty well packed. I crawled over boxes and bundles to the corner of the back seat where I was supposed to ride. Our neighbors and friends kept bringing out small bundles of food to us. Nobody here had much money or houses full of things. But whatever people had, mostly it got shared, even when the rains didn't come and we had a bad harvest. Our pueblo had had good rains this year, so the gardens were heavy with fruit and vegetables.

I put my head down against the back of the front seat and closed my eyes. There was too much to say goodbye to.

With my eyes closed, I could see my father standing there in the tall corn, looking out over the land of the pueblo. He had his flute in his hands and he made it sing.

I liked the life I knew. Without Father that life was gone.

Maybe that was why my mother was so angry.

I did not have any hope that the new life would be any better.

I missed Father more now than ever.

Chapter ✦ Three

Grandfather Whitefeather sat behind the wheel and tried to make a joke, talking like a movie Indian. "Now great metal horse take us to city of big noise!" He turned the key and looked back to see if I would think that was funny. The engine made a hiccoughing sound, rasped like a bee flying against a window, and died.

Mother sat beside him, leaning against the car door with her eyes closed, as if she did not want to look at anything anymore.

He turned the key and the car choked and gasped and then made a whirring sound that got weaker and weaker.

"I think my pony has thrown a shoe," said Grandfather. He pried open the rusty door and got out of the car.

People moved closer and watched Grandfather as he opened the hood and peered inside at the engine. Everyone was offering him advice. He fiddled around with something, then got back inside and turned the key again. A mosquito could have made a louder noise than the engine did that time.

My mother got out of the car and leaned against it. Grandfather shut the hood with a bang and went marching off toward the other side of the pueblo.

"Where you going?" my mother called out.

"Got to find somebody with a pickup to give us a tow to get it started."

"That will take too long," said Mother. She seemed in a hurry to get going, as if staying one moment longer would be painful. She waved to the people standing around, motioning for them to come, and then she mimicked a pushing action with her hand so they would know what she wanted them to do. A group of about ten men and four or five women gathered behind the car.

Grandfather leaned through the window and put the car in neutral. I started to open the door to get out, but Grandfather shook his head. "You can stay inside. You don't weigh all that much that it will make a difference."

Grandfather opened the door and my mother got in behind the wheel. "Put her in first and pop the clutch when we get it rolling," he said.

I sank back against the seat. I hoped they'd never get it started.

"Now!" cried Grandfather with a grunt. Everyone pushed, and the heavy, old car began to roll slowly forward. We hit a huge rut, and the car went crashing down on its worn-out old springs. It sagged to one side like an eagle dipping its wing to make a turn. I looked out the back window and saw strained faces as the people struggled to keep the car going. Every rut or pothole we hit seemed to break their grip on the car.

We hit a level patch and began to build up a little speed. Grandfather was holding on to the driver's-side door-frame, wheezing like an overheated rooster, his face red and drenched in sweat.

"Okay, throw in the clutch!" he gasped, limping along beside the car.

I heard the gears grind, and the car gave a big jerk. The engine started to turn over. Then we hit two or three potholes, and the car stopped dead in the ruts as if we had plowed into one of the heavy earthen walls of the pueblo.

Grandfather leaned over the door-frame, gasping for air, looking half sick.

"Maybe you should go find somebody with a pickup to give us a tow," suggested Mother.

"Why does that idea sound familiar?" asked Grandfather with a sigh. He stood up and began to limp away.

My mother got out and began talking to her friends, thanking them for helping to push. Nobody was paying any attention to me.

I'd probably never have another chance like this.

First I tried to open the rear door quietly. But it was so rusty I knew it would give me away. So instead I used the half-broken window crank and my hand to force down the back window. It went most of the way down and then got stuck a couple inches from the bottom. But that was enough space for me.

I put my hands on the roof and pulled myself out, dropped into the dust beside the car, and got down in a crouch. Nobody was looking my way. I backed up and moved around behind the car, staying low, letting it hide me from view.

Somebody was telling a funny story about Grandfather Whitefeather's old car, and while they were laughing I ran, bent low to the ground, circling off to the left as fast as I could. Nobody saw me. Soon there was plenty of brush between me and them.

Nobody was going to make me go where I didn't want to go. Nobody.

Chapter ✤ Four

I ran until I thought my legs would give out, trying to put as much distance as possible between them and me before they found out I was gone.

Hiding was not going to be easy. If my grandfather came after me, I might as well forget it. Even though he'd lived in the city for years, he was still the best tracker in the pueblo. But I was hoping he'd be too done in by the car-starting effort.

I went up to the far edge of the mesa. Maybe if I climbed up to the top, nobody would think to look for me there.

No. They would expect that. Probably the first place they'd look. People in pueblos always seem to want to hide in the high places. My father said that when he told me stories about the old days, when our people had enemies everywhere.

There was a cornfield that might make a good place to hide. Hard to see anybody crouched down among the tall corn, but they'd probably think of that, too. I could sneak back into the pueblo and maybe John Tallson, who was my best friend in the whole world, could help hide me. No, that was no good. They'd probably figure I'd go to him. Besides, someone was sure to see me if I tried to sneak back into the pueblo. No, I was on my own.

I sat down on a big old piece of red sandstone and tried to think this out. Every direction I could think of going, every place that came to mind, also seemed like a place they would likely look for me. What I had to do to avoid being found was figure out the one place nobody would expect me to go, and go there.

I got up and began to walk around, trying to think. Maybe they already knew by now that I was gone. I had moved to higher ground and from one point I could see a bend of the road. Off in the distance, I could see a battered red pickup truck putting up a cloud of dust. It was coming about as fast as you can go on roads like these and I knew it was our tow, so I didn't have much more time.

But then I *did* figure it out. They'd look for me in every direction but one, the one I didn't want to go in.

I started running again. Not back directly, but at an angle that would take me wide of them and then around the car. If I could get far enough ahead of them on the road, then dog off to the side some-where, they'd never find me.

I got down to the bend of the road before the pickup reached it, and lay down in a rain wash until the battered old truck barreled past me. I got up and began running on the road, almost chok-ing from the heavy dust the pickup had thrown up.

When I couldn't run anymore, I slowed to a walk. I was tired and would have liked to sit and rest for a while, but I needed to go a lot farther to get away.

I hoped if they couldn't find me, my mother and Grandfather Whitefeather might just go on without me. But only if they couldn't find me.

I thought my father would have wanted me to stay here. It was good enough for him; my mother should have understood that it was good enough for me.

The sun seemed to burn through the back of my head, and my boots were heavy and beginning to chafe. I'd lost track of how long I had been walk-ing. It seemed like hours, but when the sun is high in the sky, it's hard to tell exactly how much time has gone by. I should have looked at the sun when I started, to know how long I had been traveling, but I had been too busy worrying about somebody seeing me.

I saw no one. Only coyotes and roadrunners. And a Gila monster that shuffled along one side of the road, saw me, and then was gone in a flash.

I was getting thirsty. As far as I knew there was no water out in this direction. So the longer I went this way, the harder and longer it would be for me when it was time to turn around and head back. When you live in the desert you learn that you don't just wander out in it unless you plan how you're going to get to water. Without water, I couldn't stay out here all that long, not in this summer heat.

After a while the heat and thirst made me think maybe I had gone far enough. I looked around, hoping to find a good hiding place. There was a pile of broken rocks off to the left. I could scoop some sand out along one side and maybe get low enough to the ground to get some shade.

I took my shirt off and started to back slowly off the road, taking small steps and using the shirt to brush the sand smooth so no one would see where my feet left the road. I did this until I could jump up on a rock where I wouldn't leave any tracks.

I climbed in among the rocks and found a place between two big boulders that was kind of a natural resting place. There was only a little shade, but there would be more later in the afternoon.

I put my shirt back on and lay back against the rock and tried not to think about being thirsty. I shut my eyes and must have dozed off. A sound woke me.

It was the sound of a car engine with a bad muffler.

I got up slowly, moving stiffly from being cramped against the rock, and tried to sneak a look over the top of one boulder.

Grandfather Whitefeather was sitting on a small boulder. He didn't look at me, but he knew I was there. He had a battered canteen in his hands and he shook it, as if listening to the water swirling around inside.

He unscrewed the cap and took a big swig. He sighed with pleasure, made a big show of just how good the water tasted. He cupped his hand and poured some water in it and splashed it in his face. He never once looked in my direction.

When I spoke my lips felt like dried leather, they ached so bad for a taste of water.

"How did you find me?" I managed to croak.

He looked at me and almost burst out laughing. "Find you? Me? Why, I didn't even know you were lost."

I said a bad word and felt like saying even more of them. Grandfather Whitefeather seemed even more amused. "You did not learn those words from me. Perhaps your mother taught them to you."

"How did you find me?" I asked again as I crawled out from between the rocks.

"Did you want to be found?" asked Grandfather.

"You know I didn't."

"So I knew you would not hide in the usual

places. You would not seek out your friend John Tallson. You would not hide in any place that you thought we might look. This was very serious hiding out. So I stirred about and tried to be Jimmy and walk in his boots and see which way I would run in those boots."

"Maybe you'd figure out the direction, but I still don't . . ." I began, but he held up his hand.

"I know the measure of your steps in your eleventh year. How fast you walk, how hot the sun is. I know the desert in summer. I just became you and when we went down this road I tried to see a place that would be as far as you would want to go in this heat before you'd think it wise to stop."

He got up slowly, his legs creaking, and offered the canteen to me. I took it gladly and took a long, deep drink. It tasted as good as water always tastes after a long dry.

"I didn't think you would ever find me. But when you explain how you knew where to look for me, I guess you were smarter than me."

"Not smarter *than*, just as smart as you were. You thought of the most clever place to go. I just thought of it, too."

"You know I don't want to leave!" I was trapped and I knew it. Now that he had found me I had to go with them, but I didn't have to like it.

"It is not what I want or what you want, it is what your mother wants," he said patiently. "We can't talk very long now. I can't shut the car off for fear it won't start again, and if it sits too long idling it will overheat. But let me say this about the city. It is something to fear. It is both good and bad. You'll find some of both, but what is good about it, that is what your mother hopes to find for you there. Later we will talk about what those things are."

I handed him back the canteen and we began to walk slowly back in the direction of the car. I felt lower than the belly of a snake.

He put his hand on my shoulder. "I wish I could make you feel better, but I can't. I live in the city because of habit and custom. I stayed there too long and heard the song the city sings. It kind of ruined me in a way. Your father heard it, too, but he was wise in ways that I am not. Perhaps it is because I am not an educated man that I cannot go home to the pueblo and live at peace like your father did."

"I'm going to hate it," I warned him as we stepped out onto the road. I saw my mother through the car window, staring at me tight-lipped and angry.

"Try to carry the pueblo with you everywhere you go," said Grandfather Whitefeather. "Then you will have nothing to hate."

I got back in the car. I expected a big lecture from my mother, but she didn't say anything. She didn't even look back at me when Grandfather put the car into gear and we started off.

At that moment, I hated them for doing this to me. I was forced to travel and carry nothing with me.

Chapter ⁂ Five

Grandfather Whitefeather drove all the way. Mother was too upset to drive, but she never cried and she never looked back. The car was packed almost to the roof. I didn't know we had so much stuff. Later I learned most of the things were gifts from the people of the pueblo. They were generous with what little they had.

Loaded down as we were, with every pothole we hit, the frame of the car crashed down on the road. I'd been down this road before to the trading post, which is about twenty miles as the crow flies— maybe thirty if you take the road. But I'd never been beyond that except once when I was so little it hardly counts. Every time we hit a pothole I envied the crow that flies. A couple days of this and I'd have bruises.

Once we passed the trading post, I looked around a little more, hoping to see something new, anything to break the boredom I was beginning to feel. But the desert looked the same. And it stayed the same for the next eight hours.

We drove all day until Grandfather said he was too tired to drive any farther. Mother hoped we could find a motel room somewhere for the night, but the stretch of highway we were on was still too far from the main roads. So we laid out some blankets and slept under the stars.

I liked that just fine. It was almost like being home again. I didn't know if I was dreaming or just remembering how it used to be, but when I closed my eyes for the night I could see Father and Mother and myself sleeping out there under the stars. We were on the flatland beyond the farthest mesa. We'd been to a powwow a couple days' journey away, and the truck we had been riding in had broken down. We had a couple days' walk to get back home. Nobody was upset. Nobody seemed to care that we had to walk or felt like it was cursed bad luck.

It was fun, it was a chance to be alive in the world we knew, my father said.

We made snares at night and caught a jackrabbit which my father skinned and my mother cooked. My father found water, not once but twice. There was no urgency, no hurry. We just had a journey to make, and it did not matter when we got there. I can remember my father's voice, the joy that seemed to be in his words as he talked about the desert. He heard voices, in the whisper of sand and wind, in the cool earth at night giving up the heat of day.

He could talk about things I saw every day of my life and make them seem like things that had never been in the world before until he described them.

The first night, my father decided while it was still daylight that we had walked far enough, and that we should just sit and watch the day end. He said it was a good time to watch the sun go down and the stars come up, that this was how the world began and ended, and it was important to look at the night and see those things.

I remembered that and turned in my sleep or in my dream. I saw my mother sleeping in a hollowed-out depression in the sand. But where my father was supposed to be I saw a hole in the ground filled with black water, and stars were falling in it. They hissed and sizzled when they hit the water, and in the light of the falling stars, I saw my dead father floating under the surface.

I woke up. A coyote howled from a distant ridge. My mother and Grandfather Whitefeather were sleeping beside me. It was the middle of the night. I knew my father was not there and that I could not see him. I looked up at the stars. They seemed fixed in place. None of them were falling. The star that was my father had already fallen and gone out.

After a while, I drifted back to sleep and did not dream again.

When I woke up the next morning, my mother and grandfather were still asleep. I felt something stir on the blanket next to me. I moved slowly, as my father had taught me. Often we had slept out under the stars on desert nights just like this.

The thing next to me moved again.

It was a rattlesnake.

I wasn't scared. I had grown up around them. I knew the snake was only lying next to me because I was warm and he was cold. He didn't mean me any harm. My father taught me a lot about snakes. Things you don't learn in books, but only learn by living in the desert where the world is so close to you that it can teach you by touch alone.

Some people, especially white people, kill snakes on sight, but my father never did. He regarded them as good neighbors and tried to live peacefully with them. He said snakes had the same right to be alive that people had.

I carefully eased away from the rattlesnake, but it woke up. I must have made too much noise. The snake stuck its head up, looked at me for a little while, as if wondering what sort of being I was, then with dignity turned and crawled away.

I stretched and shivered. It gets cold in the morning in the desert. A hawk wheeled in the sky above us. I got up, a little stiff from sleeping on the ground, and stretched. It was hard to believe that it might be a very long time before I could sleep out under the stars again.

I stared at the sleeping forms of my mother and Grandfather Whitefeather. If there had been any place to run away to, maybe I would have tried it again. But we were in the middle of miles and miles of nowhere. It was too far to walk back, and I knew nothing about what lay ahead.

When they woke up, Grandfather was so stiff from sleeping on the ground that he almost couldn't walk. Finally we got him into the car, but Mother said she would drive. He seemed relieved but insisted only he could start the car.

Grandfather was afraid the car wouldn't start. We had only passed one other car the whole time we had been traveling on this stretch of road, so a breakdown would be a serious thing. Could be a day or more before anybody came along.

The time we had spent driving seemed to have recharged the battery, though, because when Grandfather Whitefeather turned the key, the old car roared into life. He looked relieved. He let it idle and got out and limped to the back of the car to open the trunk. He lifted a battered gas can out and went around to the side of the car, then fussed with the rag that was stuck in the end of the car's gas tank. He'd lost the gas cap that was supposed to be on it and had stuffed an old shirt in it temporarily. Grandfather finally worked the greasy shirt out and emptied the contents of the gas can into the tank.

My mother smiled. "He's had that shirt stuffed in there for four years. If that's what he means by temporary, what does he think permanent is?"

I didn't know if she was talking to me or to herself, but it was nice to see her smile over something, over anything. It was better than the look of anger that seemed to have been on her face ever since we left. She slid over into the driver's seat and waited for Grandfather to get back in.

We had intended to make a fire and heat some food for breakfast, but Mother wanted to make the trip all in two days, so we ate cold stuff while we were driving. We had deer-meat sandwiches, soggy frybread, and warm pop.

As we ate and drove, I started looking out the window with more interest. The land was less flat now, almost hilly, and the trees and brush along the road were different from any I had ever seen.

Mother looked back at me and said, "Another hour or so and we'll be in the mountains. That's the end of the desert. And once we get through the mountains, it's very different from what you're used to."

"What's it like? I mean a place without a desert?"

"You'll find out soon enough," said Grandfather.

I sank back against the hot seat. I was afraid he was right.

Chapter ᨒ Six

I had closed my eyes because the dust from the open car windows was making them itch. I must have fallen asleep.

I dreamed I was running down the road and the sun was white-hot and no matter which way I ran, when I looked back, Grandfather Whitefeather was coming right up on me in his old car. The people from the pueblo were pushing it, trying to get it started. I kept running and running and thought I would get away, but every time I looked back the car was gaining on me. It seemed like more people were helping push every time, until they were right behind me and going so fast I thought they were going to run me over. I woke up just as Grandfather's old car, with all the people of the pueblo pushing it, was about to run me down.

I had a headache from the heat and dust and from sleeping with my head against the car window. The side of my face hurt from leaning against the glass.

It was cool in the car, the heat of the day gone, and I was surprised that I had slept so long. It was almost night, but everywhere I looked I saw lights.

"Where are we?" I said, rubbing my eyes.

"We are just coming into the city. This is going to be our home," said my mother. Her voice sounded weary. She looked up at me in the rearview mirror and tried to smile.

Grandfather Whitefeather was asleep. Mother poked him a couple times until he woke up. He groaned and slowly came awake.

Mother asked him for directions, and Grandfather told her where to drive.

"Not long now, Jimmy," said Grandfather Whitefeather. He pointed through the cracked windshield. "This is your first look at a city. What do you think of it?"

I saw cars everywhere, hundreds of streets and sidewalks, and lights on almost everything. There were bars with bright neon beer signs, red and green traffic lights, and people. Lots of people. And tall buildings, some with whole sides made out of windows. No trees, no tall corn, no vegetable gardens. Just concrete everywhere.

I thought to myself, there must be some mistake. This looked like a really terrible place.

Mother turned several times on streets that Grandfather Whitefeather pointed out to her. I kept hoping that we were just driving through all this, and that where Grandfather lived would be more like where I had come from.

But we went even farther into the city. We went past the tall buildings and wide streets with four lanes of traffic, into a neighborhood where the streets were narrower and the houses were smaller and there were fewer lights.

I didn't like the looks of the really bright part of the city, but this looked even worse.

"Turn here and then it's just about four more houses," said Grandfather Whitefeather. "You can't miss it." Then, "Here. Right here," said Grandfather Whitefeather proudly. "This is my house."

We were parked at the curb in front of a tiny house that sagged. Broken rain gutters hung down from the roof on one side, and the paint was peeling around the edges. There was a small yard in front with a scraggly tree. It was the kind of house you had to live in when you had a small pension and were disabled. It was a house as ugly as the city we were in.

The house next door was all burned and blackened. The windows were boarded up and a big sign with red letters said CONDEMNED. NO TRESPASSING.

My mother was looking at me in the rearview mirror. She did not look happy. I turned my head so I did not have to look at her and stared out the window. I couldn't believe this was the street where we were supposed to live. All the houses were small, jammed almost right on top of each other. The sound of loud rock music was coming from a house across the street. There was a wrecked car in the driveway of that house, and a bunch of people sitting in the front yard drinking beer. They were laughing and shouting and making a lot of noise. The yard was full of motorcycles.

Grandfather opened the door and slowly got out. Some of the people at the party waved at him and yelled something. Whatever they were shouting did not sound friendly.

Grandfather ignored them.

"Who are those people?" I asked.

"They keep to themselves," said Grandfather with a trace of sadness. "Sometimes there is trouble. They drink and sometimes they fight and the police come. But I stay on my side of the street so they do not bother me."

We were all tired. "Let's get some sleep," my mother said. "We can unpack tomorrow."

Grandfather Whitefeather reached into the car and dragged out a small bundle. "We are not on Indian land anymore. We have to carry everything inside."

"Tomorrow morning would be soon enough," insisted Mother.

"Anything we leave in the car would be gone by morning. The city is full of thieves," said Grandfather Whitefeather.

I started dragging bundles out of the car. I was

angry, and I dumped our stuff on the sidewalk as fast as I could drag it out.

Mother and Grandfather stood beside the car. They knew I was angry, but they didn't say anything. They picked up some of our bundles and began walking to the house.

I yanked a heavy basket out of the car and it tilted and dumped gourds and squash all over the lawn. I was so angry I kicked one of the big gourds that my mother had hollowed out and used for storage. It rolled into the street. A car came down the street and its rear wheels hit the gourd and smashed it.

I turned and looked back to see if they had noticed what had happened. My grandfather was using a key to open the front door. My mother was sitting on the front steps of the house. She was crying.

I felt sorry for her and wished I could make her feel better. So I stopped being angry and made them both stay in the house and rest. They were so tired they let me do it. I brought all of our stuff inside. My arms were aching and my back was sore, but I felt better. It was good to have something to do, better than just sitting there and thinking about how awful everything seemed. I thought they were both glad I carried the stuff in.

Since my father was gone, maybe now I was the one who was supposed to carry things.

Chapter ✵ Seven

I had a room of my own. It had a fairly good bed, soft when I bounced on it. There was a table lamp that worked and two wooden dressers with enough drawers for me to store all my clothes and stuff. There was a big, old green chair in one corner, the kind that lets you sink in until you feel it is wrapped around you. There was even a radio on a wall shelf. I turned it on and it worked.

I had never had a radio before. I twisted the dial. There must have been a hundred stations on it, and some of them were playing real strange kinds of music. It didn't sound much like country music to me.

Some people back at the pueblo had radios, the kind that work on batteries. But we lived so far away from anything we could only get one station real good and sometimes another one if the sky was clouded up over the mesas.

My mother wanted to fix me something to eat before I went to bed, but I could tell she was bone tired and just wanted to sleep. I was hungry but I was in no mood to talk to anyone about anything, so I figured it was better to be hungry up in my room than downstairs with an earful and a bellyful.

I was going to unpack and put my stuff away, but that would make it seem like we really were going to stay here. Leaving it packed meant there was still time to change our minds and go back. It was hard to imagine living here for a day, let alone forever. I didn't want to even think about that.

I slammed the door to my room. It had a lock on it so I locked it. Mother and Grandfather were still moving around downstairs, shifting stuff around and talking. They both sounded pretty beat.

I hadn't looked around the house much. It was two stories, sort of. My room was the only one up-stairs. It was pretty narrow and the ceiling slanted in from both sides, so it must have been an attic that somebody made into a room. There was a tiny window, just one, so I went over and looked out. As I'd thought, there was nothing to see, just another house only a few feet away. I pulled the curtain shut.

Our house in the pueblo had lots of windows, some to let in the morning sun and some set to catch the way the sky looks at twilight. The sun

34

always came into the house from somewhere. When you looked out the windows, it seemed as if you could see a hundred miles between the mesas. The air was clear and pure and seemed to go on forever. Not like this dump. Why bother to even have a window if there's nothing to look at?

Once I'd closed the curtain, I just sat on the bed and tried to think. Then suddenly I got real panicky. The walls seemed to be closing in on me. I didn't know why, but this room was really getting to me. Then I realized it was because I wasn't used to having a door. Before, I'd just had a blanket separating my room from the rest of the house.

With the locked door and closed curtain, this room felt like a prison. I jumped up, unlocked the door, and swung it open. It only opened onto the landing at the top of the stairs but even that made me feel a whole lot better. I went back to the window, pulled back the curtain, and opened it. Still nothing to look at, but at least there was some air.

I got undressed and crawled into bed. The sheets were stiff and didn't seem very practical. I was used to blankets, mostly—a heavy one under me and a thinly woven one for a top cover. I had a blanket in a sack with some of my stuff, so I ripped the sheets off the bed and tossed them aside. I got out the red-and-blue blanket with the thunderbird dancing on it that my aunt had made for me. I wrapped myself up in it and felt a little better. At least it was something from home. A home I didn't have anymore.

I curled up and tried to sleep.

I was used to the sounds of the desert, the whispers of sand blowing against the sagebrush, the soft rustle of night animals making their way through the cacti and desert shrubs. I missed the soft hooting of the hunting owl, the lonely cry of the coyote high up on the mesas. I tried to imagine I heard all those things again so I could sleep.

I heard cars moving out in the street in front of the house. There seemed to be as many of them as there were fish in a river. I heard sirens like the ones I'd heard sometimes on state police cars when there was trouble and they came out to the pueblo. I heard other kinds of sirens, too, maybe fire trucks, which I had read about but never seen, or ambulances. I heard loud music playing, people shouting and laughing, and once the unmistakable crash of broken glass and somebody saying a lot of bad words. I heard dogs barking, but quiet, as if they were locked up inside a house and the sound came through the walls.

And always I heard the cars going by. None of those sounds made me comfortable. I had gotten an earful, but I slept like a star fallen out of the sky.

Chapter ❦ Eight

I woke up early, long before morning, feeling restless. When I looked out my window I saw it was still dark outside and not getting much lighter. I had no real reason to be up at that time of the night, but I had done all the sleeping I intended to do.

I got up quietly and went downstairs and cleaned up in the bathroom, carrying my boots in my hands, tiptoeing around so I wouldn't wake anybody. I was so hungry I could have eaten something that was still moving. But it could wait.

I stood outside the door of the room my mother was sleeping in but didn't hear anything. I walked real quiet past a small room with an open door. Grandfather Whitefeather was stretched out in there on a small, wooden army cot. I guessed he gave my mother his room and was sleeping in there temporarily. If I knew Grandfather, he probably would sleep in there temporarily for the rest of his life.

I moved real quiet but got the feeling Grandfather was awake and knew I was up and moving around. I hesitated, wondering if I should go or not. It wasn't like I really knew where I was going; I just wanted to get out of the house. Get away from them for a while, see a little of what there was to see.

I went out the front door, carefully pulled it shut behind me, and sat down on the front steps to put my boots on.

I shivered. It was colder than I expected. I just had an old T-shirt on and wished I had thought to bring a coat. I kept forgetting that we weren't in the desert anymore and that everything was going to be different, even the weather.

Out on the sidewalk, I wondered which way to go. Right, the street seemed to lead only to more houses. But to the left, a few streets down it looked like stores and shops, so I decided to go that way.

It was very early, more night than morning, but I was used to being up before the sun began its march across the sky. Apparently not many people in the city were up at that time of night. Some of the houses had lights on but most were still dark. The stores were half-lit, most with CLOSED signs on them. There were stores that sold lamps, a hardware store, several Mexican restaurants, some fast-food hamburger places, carpet stores, liquor stores, insurance offices, and something called a thrift store that had old furniture and clothes hanging in the window.

Some of the stores had broken windows with big pieces of plywood nailed over them, and most had heavy iron bars around the windows and doors. They looked like they were in prison. What kind of place was this that they had to put the stores in cages?

Nobody passed me on the street. I seemed to be the only one up. Cars went up and down the street but not many of them. I didn't know what time it was, but morning seemed quite a ways off.

I missed the pueblo, and the more I walked around and the more I saw, the more I hated being here. The streets were dirty, the stores were run down, and it seemed like the kind of place where no one could ever be happy.

I came to an intersection. There were more stores down this other street, and some of them seemed to be open. At the end of the block a gas-station sign was flashing on and off and a car was filling up at the pump. Across from the station was a coffee shop with a big sign that said OPEN 24 HOURS.

I went down that street and looked in the window of the restaurant. A couple of old men were sitting at a long counter in the front of the place, drinking coffee.

The door opened and a man came out, toward me. His hair was long and greasy, he smelled bad, and his hands were trembling. I moved back a few steps. He stopped in front of me, staring at me as if I was in the way.

"Hey kid, you got any smokes?"

I could barely understand him.

"Give me a cigarette! You gotta cigarette? I'm outta smokes!" He stumbled toward me menacingly. I edged away.

"S'matter you little punk, I won't hurt ya," said the man. "You got any spare change?"

Sometimes one makes a gift of tobacco to one's elders, but it's done out of respect. This was an old man but also a stranger. Why was he asking me for tobacco?

His breath smelled of whiskey. He sneered at me, and I saw his teeth were bad.

"I don't have anything," I said.

He made a motion as if to hit me and when I flinched, stumbled on past. "Stupid kid!" snarled the man. "Outta my way!"

I wondered if he was an example of the kind of people I would meet here in the city. This was not a friendly place. I felt maybe a hundred times worse and wished I had stayed in my room. Nothing I would see out here would make me feel any better about being here. I turned around and started walking back to my grandfather's house.

"Hey, you!" somebody shouted at me.

I turned my head. A man sitting in a police car was rolling down his window. He looked angry about something. He motioned me to come to him.

I didn't know why he wanted to talk to me, but I went over.

He got out of his car. He wore a dark-blue uniform and his face was harsh and red; he had a short stick in one hand and a flat notebook on a clipboard in the other. The policeman kept tapping the stick against the side of his leg as if he was nervous.

"Where do you think you're going?" he said, sounding very unfriendly.

"Back to my grandfather's house," I said.

"Where you coming from?"

"The same place," I said, not knowing where else I would have come from unless he meant the pueblo.

"How old are you?" Every question he asked seemed angry, as if everything about me was somehow wrong.

"Why are you out here at this time of night in this neighborhood? What the devil are you up to anyway?"

He didn't even give me time to answer.

"You run away from home?"

I didn't know which question to answer first.

"Your parents know where you are?"

"No."

"Just what I thought!" He beckoned with the stick, motioning for me to come closer.

I stepped toward him reluctantly, wondering what the stick was for. I hoped he wasn't going to hit me with it.

He shifted the notebook out of his hand, set it down on the car roof, and grabbed me by the shoulder.

"Okay, kid, you come with me."

He was holding me so tight it hurt. He forced me to walk around to the other side of the car, opened the door, and shoved me inside. "Just sit there, kid. Don't you dare make a move." He came around, got his notebook, and got back in on his side of the car.

"Am I being arrested?" Maybe I had done something wrong, but I didn't know what. I was getting scared.

He took out his clipboard, unsnapped a pen from his shirt pocket, and began to write. He didn't look at me, just asked for my name, age, and the name of my parents and my grandfather. I told him all that and he wrote it down. He asked me at what address I was staying in the city. I didn't know it.

"What do you mean you don't know it, a kid eleven years old? What are you trying to give me?" Now he was angry again.

I explained that we had just moved here, that I didn't know the name of the street but knew how to walk back. He acted like everything I said was a lie.

"You're not going to walk back anywhere this time of night. I'll take you back and you better have your story straight by the time we get there. I'm not going to be happy, kid, if you're shoveling me a lot of snow."

I didn't know what he meant about the snow, but I knew he did not like me.

He made me fasten my seat belt, and he talked on the radio to someone and told them where he was and what he was doing. Then he started the car and drove me back to my grandfather's house.

"There. That one," I said.

"Hope you ain't lying," said the policeman.

Why would he think I would lie about something like that? I did not understand this policeman or why he seemed so angry all the time. Maybe he hated Indians.

"Am I under arrest?"

"Did you do something you ain't told me about, like rob a bank?" He grinned when he said it, and then I wondered if he was making fun of me.

I shook my head no.

"Could have sworn you looked like a bank robber," said the cop, unbuckling his seat belt. He reached over and unsnapped mine. "Get out, kid."

I opened the door and he got out the same time I did. I could see lights on in my grandfather's house. Mother and Grandfather were up and probably wondering where I was.

"Can I go now if I'm not arrested?"

"Not without me. I give door-to-door service," he said. "Besides, we ain't done yet."

We went up to the front door. I started to open it, but he pulled me back and then knocked on the door. He didn't have to do that, I knew, because it was unlocked.

Grandfather Whitefeather and my mother both came to the door. They looked relieved to see me, but uneasy at seeing the policeman there.

"What's the trouble, Officer?" asked Grandfather Whitefeather.

"You tell me," said the policeman. "I found him walking on the corner of Calumet and Clay streets at 4:38 in the morning. A kid this young's got no business being down there that time of night, but you all should know that, right?"

My mother spoke up for me. "He's lived in a pueblo all his life. He's never been in a city before. He just doesn't know any better."

"Now's the time to teach him," said the policeman with a grim look on his face. "There's a world of trouble out there for somebody who doesn't know what's what."

"What did I do?"

"You want me to tell him?" said the policeman, looking at his watch, acting eager to get going. "Or can I trust you folks to put him straight?"

"We'll explain it to him, Officer," said Grandfather Whitefeather. "And thank you for seeing that he got safely back to us."

"No problem," said the policeman. He pointed a finger at my mother and grandfather. "Just see that it doesn't happen again." He nodded a kind of goodbye, turned, and went back to his car.

I could tell everybody was upset with me.

"C'mon into the kitchen," said my mother. "I've got some food for you."

"And I've got some good advice for you. Now's as good as any time for it," said Grandfather Whitefeather.

I ate corncakes and drank some apple juice. My mother sat in her chair and did not eat much. My grandfather finished his food as quickly as he could. It was plain he wanted to tell me things.

"You talk to him," my mother said to Grandfather. "You know how to say it best. You know how it is here better than me."

"Jimmy," Grandfather began. "In the daytime, when you know your way around, there are a lot of places you can walk to, things to see. But *only* in the daytime. This is not the pueblo. At night there you can go for long walks in any direction. You can sit out on the mesa and listen to the coyotes if you cannot sleep."

I drank more juice. It didn't taste good. Nothing here did.

"But you can't go out here alone at night. It's very dangerous. You have to stay in this house. This neighborhood is not safe. Even I do not walk here after dark. That is just the way it is."

"Why was the policeman so angry with me? Does he hate Indians?"

"I don't know what he does or doesn't hate," said Grandfather Whitefeather. "He was just doing his job. He was protecting you, seeing to it that you got home safe and that we knew where you were."

"This isn't a house, it's a prison," I said.

"I promise you," said my mother. "It seems bad

and strange and very different from what you are used to, but you will find things that you like here. It *will* have good things, too!"

I wanted to believe her. But it sounded like the kind of story people tell kids just to make them feel better. Not that I thought she was lying. She never lies. But sometimes she says things because she hopes they will be true even if they aren't.

I was still hungry, but too angry with them for bringing me here to ask for more corncakes.

"You know what things in the desert are dangerous, don't you?" said Grandfather Whitefeather.

I nodded yes.

"Did you always know it?"

I shrugged. "Well, no. I guess I learned it."

Then I knew what he was getting at.

"Just like the desert has its own dangers, the scorpions that crawl in your shoes at night, the washes that flashflood when it storms in the mountains, this place has its own dangers. When you have learned to deal with them then you will be able to live in this city desert, too."

My mother smiled at me. "Listen to your grandfather. You could not ask for a better guide."

She scooped up two corncakes and slid them on my plate.

"And eat before your shadow becomes bigger than you are."

I ate, but it didn't make me feel any better.

Chapter ❧ Nine

My mother found a job. Not right away, but after about a week of looking. It was only washing dishes at a restaurant, and she said it didn't pay real good, but it was a start.

My grandfather tried to get me to go with him and look at the neighborhood. He said he would take me to see the school that I would go to in the fall, but I told him I wasn't interested. I came down for meals but mostly I stayed up in my room.

They were trying hard to make me comfortable, but nothing they could do or say was going to do that. I was dying of boredom up in my room, endlessly dialing through the radio stations, listening to all kinds of things that I didn't much like or understand.

One morning at breakfast I was just sitting there,

staring at my corncakes and breakfast cereal, neither of which I felt like eating.

My mother was leaving for work. She had a brown uniform on.

"I have good news," she said.

I didn't look at her.

"My boss is gonna let me try waitressing, starting today."

"Is that better?" I still wasn't looking at her.

"I'm hoping it is. There's extras that go with it. This is only temporary, but it'll mean more money for sure. One of the regular waitresses has an illness in the family. She had to go to Tucson."

"That is hard work," said Grandfather Whitefeather.

"More complicated maybe, but no harder than washing dishes," said my mother, looking pleased at the prospect. "I get a small raise in pay and I get tips. Flora, that's the cashier, says a waitress can make half as much as her salary just on tips!"

"That's a good sign. Don't you think so, Jimmy?" asked Grandfather Whitefeather, hoping I would seem pleased for my mother's sake.

"Big deal," I said.

"Jimmy, you're going to have to get over being angry with us," said my mother firmly. "We're here to stay. I'm going to make a life for us here. I have my reasons and you just better decide to make the best of it."

She rummaged through her old, black purse and

came out with a couple of quarters. "Here. Buy yourself some ice cream. Grandfather will show you where you can get it."

She knew I liked ice cream. It was one of my favorite things to buy at the trading post. But I wouldn't take the money.

My mother looked sad, standing there with her hand out. Finally she put the money back in her purse and looked at my grandfather, as if it was somehow up to him now.

"Jimmy, I can't stay and argue with you. I have to go now or I'll be late for work. We need to talk this out. Tonight when I come home, we'll do that, I promise."

She squared her shoulders, looking uncomfortable in the stiff uniform, and went out the front door. I heard the sound of Grandfather's old car starting up and her driving away. I just stared at my food.

"Your mother is in a lot of pain, Jimmy. She's trying to do what is best. She is doing all her heart will allow. Try to think of her, Jimmy, of how she feels. If you keep acting this way, you will break her heart."

"I don't care!" I pushed the plate of food away and started to get up from the table.

"Yes you do. You may tell that lie to yourself, but if you think about it for a little while, even you don't believe it."

"She had no right to bring me here!" I said angrily.

He seemed to think about that for a while, as if trying to decide to speak of something he did not want to talk about. Finally, with a worried look on his face, he said, "It is a promise she made your father. It is not for me to say more."

"My father wanted me to come here? I don't believe it. You're lying!"

"It is not my place to tell you about it. When it is time, your mother will tell you what she promised your father."

"I don't believe you. My father would never have wanted me to be in this crummy place!" I stood up, ready to go back to my room.

Grandfather got up slowly and began to clear away the dishes.

"It is too nice a day to be hiding in your room. Come out and help me mow the yard. I have one of those push mowers without a motor, and I think you could learn to run it."

"I'm busy. I don't have time for stupid stuff like that," I said, not looking at him, and went on upstairs. I knew I was acting hateful but didn't know how to stop.

I sat there for a long time, feeling bored and useless. I could see the sun shining bright from my window, and I was curious to see how a push lawn mower worked. Nobody had one out in the desert because nobody had a lawn. I was feeling guilty, too. I knew he wanted me to help him because his legs were hurting.

I heard the front door open and then I saw Grandfather Whitefeather go around to the back of the house. There was a whirring sound, and I stuck my head out the window to see what it was.

He was pushing a two-wheeled thing with spinning blades across the lawn slowly, favoring his bad leg. The grass whirled out behind the mower in a spray of green. It was kind of neat to watch.

I wanted to go down and try it out, but I'd already been so mean about it I couldn't think of any way to go back on what I said without feeling foolish.

Grandfather Whitefeather looked up and saw me watching him. He smiled up at me, and I felt even worse. I was hoping he might fall, his bad leg maybe giving out on him, so I could rush down and take over, but he just kept limping back and forth across the lawn.

He stopped abruptly and looked up at me.

"Jimmy, my legs are hurting real bad. Are you sure you couldn't come down and try this for a minute or so, or until I get my strength back?"

I smiled and fairly flew down the stairs.

He let me take the handles and push. The mower made a neat *whir whir* and the cut grass just came shooting up at me. I really put my legs into it and tried to make it go as fast as I could run.

Grandfather Whitefeather sat down on an old chair. I could tell he was glad I had taken over for him. "That's it! Now you got it! Make her sing, Jimmy!"

I ran until I was out of breath and out of grass, too. Then he made me stop because he said I was mowing some of it two or three times, and he didn't want to spoil the grass into thinking it was going to get that kind of attention every week.

It felt good to run and move and be outside instead of being a jailbird up in my room. The sun was warm on my back and I liked the smell of the fresh-cut grass. Somehow it smelled like summer.

Later I let Grandfather take me out to buy some ice cream. It tasted just as good as it used to taste when we got it at the trading post. Grandfather said it was because some things are good no matter where you are. Their goodness travels to every place that you do.

We were talking about ice cream, but I knew he was talking about more than that.

It was almost a good day.

Chapter ✸ Ten

The first week in the city, we still ate as though we were living in the pueblo. We had so many vegetables people had given us—good yellow squash, fresh tomatoes, and corn—that we didn't need any other food. If I closed my eyes while eating, I could almost think I was back home.

Once the lawn was done, I was bored again. But my grandfather had something else for us to do. While I was putting the lawn mower away on the back porch, he opened a tool shed and rummaged around inside. He moved some stuff around so he could get to something, and then he dragged out a small, four-wheeled red wagon.

He called it his bring-'em-back wagon. Before he had had a car, he'd used the wagon to go to the store and bring back food. He said now that Mother was using the car, it was up to us to shop for some groceries.

We were running out of coffee, which I don't drink but my mother and grandfather can't live without. And we needed sugar and other stuff.

I pulled the wagon and we walked for a ways, not saying anything much. We passed a small store that was about the size of the trading post back home. It sold beer and soda pop and some groceries, but we went right on past.

"That's what they call a convenience store," said Grandfather Whitefeather. "It has milk and eggs and a few other things, but what we want is the supermarket. It's not much farther."

"It looks like a trading post," I said. I couldn't understand why we would walk by a store that sold food to find another store that did the same thing.

"Shortcut," said Grandfather, and we turned in the middle of one street and went down an alley. At the end of the alley, we came into the parking lot of a huge building. It was the biggest store I had ever seen.

We walked up to the front door and it popped open before we could even touch it. I jumped, but Grandfather seemed to think doors were supposed to do that so he walked on ahead. I shrugged and went in behind him, pulling the wagon.

I looked back and saw other people walking up to the door. It opened for them, too. Maybe there was somebody hiding somewhere who was pulling a string and opening the door when people came up to it. I reminded myself to ask Grandfather about it later.

I turned around and looked at the supermarket. I had never seen so many things to eat in one place in my whole life. There couldn't possibly be that many kinds of food in the whole world! We walked down one row and it was all fruits and vegetables. Just this one row was as wide as a horse corral and as long as the whole plaza in the center of the pueblo. They had apples, but not just one kind like the trading post had. They had at least ten different kinds, some red, and some yellow, and some green ones that must not have been ripe.

And there was row after row full of canned goods and food packages and boxes, even one whole row with nothing but breakfast cereal in it. I thought there were only four or five different kinds of cereal in the whole world because that's all the trading post ever carried. But here there were hundreds and hundreds of different kinds of cereal. If you had the money, you could eat something different for breakfast every day. We went past a couple dozen rows before we even started down the one with the fruits and vegetables. I just couldn't get over how many things were on the shelves.

It was so big it was scary.

I must have been standing there with my mouth open because Grandfather Whitefeather turned to look at me and then started laughing.

"I forgot. You've never seen a supermarket before, have you?"

I shook my head no.

"Think of it this way," said Grandfather as he put some hot peppers in a plastic bag. "This store is speaking to you. It is telling you some of the things that your mother wants you to learn."

I didn't understand.

"A trading post in the pueblo only shows you a small part of the world. This store speaks of a world that is a very big place."

"So I should just forget where we come from, is that it?"

"No. Carry it with you, so that you may be always in both worlds, large and small."

"So it's big, so what! I'd rather be in a trading post any old day. Maybe they only have one kind of apple, but they are all ripe!" While I was saying that I was watching a woman putting the green apples into a bag. "That woman is being cheated because she doesn't know the apples aren't ripe."

Grandfather laughed again. He walked over to the table where the green apples were and put about half a dozen of them in a sack. He put the plastic bag in the wagon with the bag of peppers.

"You'll get a bellyache if you eat green apples," I said.

Grandfather Whitefeather looked as though he were going to laugh again, but he didn't.

We didn't talk much after that. I trailed along

while Grandfather Whitefeather filled the cart with what we needed. I saw lots of new things. I was burning to ask him what those strange foods were and what they tasted like and where they came from, but I remembered I was supposed to be bored and not interested in anything so I didn't speak about it.

When we were ready to leave, we went up to pay. There were seven or eight cash registers. This store was a real busy place! At the trading post there was one cash box and you had to bring your own baskets or boxes for the stuff you bought.

Grandfather paid his money, and the woman rang it up and then packed his groceries in paper bags. A young man in a white shirt put them in the wagon for us. Nobody said much, and nobody talked about the weather or the corn crops or who had an illness in the family. At the trading post sometimes you can spend longer talking at the cash box than you do picking out your groceries. But the woman rang up our stuff real quick, with just a nod of her head to Grandfather, and the guy who bagged up our groceries was in a hurry, too. As soon as our stuff was in the wagon, they were busy with another customer.

Grandfather seemed to act like this was what he expected so I didn't say anything. Maybe everybody in a city always acted like strangers. I remembered the policeman. Maybe that was how people got along with each other here.

When we got outside, I was pulling the wagon and Grandfather was smiling as if he understood some private joke. About halfway back, he motioned for me to stop. He bent over and rummaged around in the bags until he found the plastic bag with the green apples.

"Feel like sharing an apple with me?"

I was hungry, but I shook my head no. A green-apple stomachache is just about the worst kind there is. Even a horse won't eat green apples.

Grandfather Whitefeather pulled out one apple and used a small pocketknife he took out of his shirt pocket to cut it in half. He bit into one section of the apple and offered me the other piece. He chewed, making a great show of how good it tasted.

"Not afraid of an apple, are you?"

I shrugged. I didn't know why he was making such a big deal over an apple, so I took it. It was kind of big for an unripe apple. I bit into it and it was juicy and sweet.

"It's not a trick. I thought it was when I saw them, too. But it is some kind of apple from a far-off place called New Zealand, and it gets ripe but it stays green." He finished his half of the apple and looked to see how I was liking mine.

"It tastes pretty good," I finally admitted. I was still surprised. I took another bite, wishing my friends back in the pueblo could see this. A green apple that was ripe! It just didn't seem possible somehow.

"You're going to see lots of new things here. Just try not to forget the old things you already know and you will do well," said Grandfather.

We shared another apple before we got back to the house. We went pretty slow because Grandfather's legs were aching. He said pushing the lawn mower made them hurt. I said I wouldn't mind running the lawn mower for him, just to save his legs. He seemed pretty happy about that and gave me another apple to eat later.

I was happy, too, for a while. Not much but a little bit. I sat out on the fresh-mown grass, thinking about how good the green apple had tasted. I rubbed the one Grandfather had given me on the front of my shirt until the skin shone like a green marble. I took a bite, and it was just as good as any ripe apple ever gets.

Then I wondered if my father had ever had one of these ripe, green apples. The fruit seemed to lose its flavor. I spit it out and threw the rest of it away. I lay back down on the grass and just looked up at the sky.

The sun was still shining, but it didn't shine for me.

Chapter ✣ Eleven

When my mother got home that night I knew it had been a day without sun for her, too.

Grandfather and I were sitting in the kitchen when she came through the front door. She looked at us as if we had done something wrong.

"I suppose you are hungry and waiting for me to cook something!" she said, looking harried. Her eyes were red, and I knew she had been crying.

"I have a stew on the stove. By the time you wash up and change out of your restaurant clothes, it should be ready," said Grandfather calmly. "I have sugared apples baking in the oven for dessert."

She didn't say anything more, just marched out of the kitchen and went into her room. I heard her banging things around as she changed clothes.

"Storm weather," said Grandfather and smiled at

me. "It is up to us to be cheerful so she will forget about the clouds."

But she was in no better mood when she came out and we all sat down to eat. It was a silent meal. Mother seemed so angry that it was just better to let her alone. But I was curious, and the silence was beginning to get to me.

"How did your new job as a waitress go?" I asked as I ladled a second helping of stew onto my plate.

Grandfather sighed and looked at me sadly. I suppose I should have kept quiet, but it was too late. My mother put down her fork and looked at me directly and I wished I hadn't asked.

"They humiliated me. The customers complained that I was slow and stupid. That I forgot things, that I brought the wrong orders and I was too slow to refill their coffee cups. All morning long that is how it went."

"The first day of every job is hard," said Grandfather Whitefeather. "Tomorrow will be better. Each day it will get better. Things that are hard for you will become easy over time."

"There won't be a tomorrow. There were so many complaints the owner made me go back into the kitchen to wash dishes. He was angry with me all day."

"I am sorry," said Grandfather.

"I don't blame them," said Mother, but it was plain she did. "I was slow. I did not know what half the things they ordered were. I did not know that a sunny-side up was a way to fix an egg and that hashbrowns were not meat but some way to make potatoes. I couldn't tell one dish from the other."

"But it's not your fault if you didn't know," I said, sticking up for her.

"No. It was my fault. I got things all mixed up. I kept having to ask each customer what it was he was ordering. Then I was taking too long and the customers were in a hurry and not friendly. Not knowing things is never a good enough excuse. That is something you learn here very quickly."

"If they had given you time to learn those things, then you could have done as well as anyone," said Grandfather.

"I learned that no one has time for anything," said my mother bitterly. "But then it is not the first time or the last time in my life that I have been treated this way." She hesitated and then looked at Grandfather. "And you know, I have been treated worse."

He nodded as if he understood all too well, lowered his eyes, and looked away. It was as if they shared a secret and didn't want to talk about it. They looked over at me suddenly, as if it had something to do with me. I saw a look of such sadness pass over my mother's face that it brought a lump to my throat. Nobody said anything but everybody felt bad.

Finally, my grandfather set his fork down with a loud bang and said with an attempt at cheerfulness, "You are home now, try not to think of it."

My mother shook her head. "I can't help it. My

boss said I must be lazy. He hung around the kitchen all day to see if I was even good enough to wash dishes. He didn't say that was what he was doing, but I knew. I had to work harder than I ever did before. I went as fast I could all day, until my arms ached so bad I could hardly stand it. All just so I could keep the simple job I started with."

"Eat and I will bring you a better time," said Grandfather. "I stand on the mesa and dream that I am in a better place. Come with me and we shall go to that better day."

She smiled then, reached out, and took his hand. She closed her eyes and let Grandfather begin to talk about that day.

It was not a game, it was a part of how they sometimes ended a day. She and Grandfather had done the same thing when my father was sick. They would hold hands and close their eyes, and Grandfather would remember a happy day and they would dream they were in it.

Grandfather said they traveled to a time when Father was not sick, and they would find something to make the heart glad. At first I took part, in those early days, and I must have really believed in Grandfather's dreaming then. But it didn't change anything. It didn't make my father well again. Mother said it gave her comfort, but it only made me so lonesome for my father I wanted to cry.

Now Grandfather began to talk about a day when it rained in the mountains and the clouds walked so low to the ground they seemed to dance over the earth. My mother described the sky, pure and sweet with the smell of rain, and talked about her neighbors as if they were right there in the room with her. They were gone, dream-walking, and for who knew how long.

My mother was supposed to have a talk with me tonight. But they were back at the pueblo now. Grandfather had reshaped a dream of home with his hands like a carver who finds a hidden animal face in dark wood. They were not thinking about me or their dinner, which was getting cold on their plates.

I took a piece of bread and my plate with my second helping of stew and went to my room. They didn't notice I left and probably didn't care. I didn't want to be around them when they were like this. It was okay if they wanted to try to dream away a bad day, but it didn't work for me. I just had to live through bad days the way they were.

Besides, if they missed the pueblo that much, if all the good days were back there, why were we staying in this stupid place? Grandfather said it was because of some promise my mother had made to my father, but nobody would ever get me to believe that. This had to be the last place my father would ever want me to be.

It made no sense and it made me angry. We were here, but nobody had a good reason why.

I'd run away, but this city was just too big a desert.

Chapter ✢ Twelve

I mowed the yard again after the grass had a week to grow. It was fun. At least it was something to do.

I went walking a few times with my grandfather, but there wasn't much I wanted to see. We went into the thrift store one afternoon. I had a little money my mother had given me and almost bought a book about horses. I had to choose between that and ice cream, and the ice cream won out.

There were some kids my age who lived on my street, but I didn't try to talk to them and they didn't try to talk to me. Grandfather said I'd make friends as soon as summer was over and school started.

My mother came home every night strained and tired. Her hands were red and the skin on her fingers looked raw from all the hot water they used to wash the dishes. Grandfather gave her a pine-needle lotion, but it didn't seem to help.

I got fed up one day with doing nothing, so I went off exploring. Grandfather had fallen asleep in an old chair in the living room so no one was around to stop me. I decided to walk as far as I could go in one direction. Maybe I would see something interesting, maybe I wouldn't. At least it was something to do.

I walked a long way, but walking on the sidewalk was a lot harder than walking on sand. I came to a very different neighborhood than the one we lived in. The stores were bigger here and brighter and the houses were twice the size of Grandfather's.

After a while my heels began to hurt and my boots felt tight. So I stopped and sat down on the sidewalk in front of a store and took my boots and socks off to rest my feet. People walking by turned their heads and stared at me. I got the feeling they thought I was doing something wrong, but I couldn't figure out what it could possibly be.

I leaned against the store window and closed my eyes. The sun was shining on this side of the street and it felt good and warm on my face. I stretched out and got comfortable. It felt nice to rest.

Somebody tapped me on the shoulder. I opened my eyes and several people were crowded around. A white-haired man and woman were bending over me, looking at me like they were real worried about something.

"Are you all right?" asked the woman.

"Sure," I said, starting to sit up.

"Are you ill?" she insisted.

"Oh, June, I think he looks okay to me," the man said to her, glancing at his watch, as if he had someplace else where he wanted to be.

"I'm fine," I said. I pulled my socks back on and starting sliding into my boots. I was embarrassed that these people were standing there staring at me. "I was just resting my feet."

"Where are you from?"

I knew the address by now so I told them.

"He looks sick to me," said the woman. "Listen, if you're not feeling well, maybe we can help. Have you had anything to eat?"

"For heaven's sake!" said the man, who must have been her husband. "We don't know if he's homeless or hungry or sick or anything."

"I had a big meal about an hour ago," I insisted. They seemed very friendly but nervous.

"Where are your folks?" said the woman, ignoring her husband.

"My mother's at work. My grandfather is sleeping." For people who didn't know me, they sure asked a lot of questions.

"What would your mother think about you sleeping in the street?" asked the woman, sounding stern now and not so friendly.

"I wasn't sleeping. I was just resting."

"You shouldn't do that. The street is no place for

sleeping," said the woman. "But you look like a nice young man and I hope you will understand that this is not charity!" She put one hand in her purse and pulled out a thick wad of paper money. She picked out four one-dollar bills and tried to hand them to me. I just stared at her, not knowing what to think.

"Really. Take it. It's yours. Maybe you are ashamed to admit you're hungry, but it's really okay. Here. Take it!" She moved closer so the money was almost in my face.

"If he doesn't want it—" the man began impatiently.

"He wants it," she said. "Just look at his clothes. The poor thing."

I didn't know what else to do, with everybody staring at me, so I took the money. I folded it up and put it in my jeans.

"Thank you very much," I said.

"Glad to help," said the woman as her husband took her by the arm and began to lead her away. "Now you see that you buy food with that, you hear?"

I watched them walk away. Then I called out to her.

"Why did you give me this money?"

She turned and looked back. "Because you are poor," she said as they stopped beside a big, white car.

"I am not poor!" I yelled back at her, remembering the things my father had always said. "I am Indian!"

Her husband unlocked the car door and she started to get in. She called out, "Well, dear, it's the same thing!" She ducked inside the car and they drove off.

I started to walk back home. It was nice to have some money, but I didn't feel I had earned it. I knew I could buy some ice cream and that I could go back to the thrift store and buy the book on horses. I probably could even get something to eat to bring home to my mother and grandfather.

But it did not feel right somehow. As I walked along I wondered why the woman had acted the way she had. It took me most of the way home to figure it out. She wasn't really friendly. She didn't like me or want to know me.

She just felt sorry for me.

When I opened the front door to Grandfather's house and looked inside, it seemed small and dark and a million miles from everything I cared about.

And I knew that I felt sorry for myself, too.

Chapter ✦ Thirteen

My mother was waiting for me by the door, and she looked both angry and scared.

"Where have you been?" She was almost yelling.

"Nowhere. I just went for a walk." I was going to tell her about the woman and the four dollars, but she didn't give me a chance.

"Walking where? How far did you go? Did you leave this street? Haven't we told you time and time again not to go off until you know where everything is? Can't you mind us? We were worried sick about you!"

"I wasn't gone all that long and besides—"

"Your grandfather is out in the car looking for you! You didn't tell him where you were going. He thought you ran away. Dinner has been ready for more than an hour. And we won't eat until Grandfather gets back. You have him worried sick! You ought to be ashamed of yourself!"

It didn't seem like all that big a deal at first but then I felt bad for causing all this trouble. I wished I'd told them what I had meant to do.

"I was real careful not to get lost, but I'm sorry I made you worry so much. I didn't mean to upset you."

"Go wash up and then wait in your room until he gets back. I doubt if supper will be fit to eat by then, but you'll eat it even if it's burned to a crisp!"

Plenty of times I was late for meals in the pueblo and nobody ever made such a big noise about it. I could take care of myself anyway—I am eleven, after all. It wasn't like I was four years old or something! I went up and sat on my bed. Maybe I'd just stay up here and never come down.

I heard Grandfather's noisy, old car pull into the driveway. If I hadn't been so hungry, maybe I would have just stayed in my room, but after all that walking, I could have eaten two burned dinners.

"Come to dinner!" my mother yelled up the stairs.

I went down to the kitchen. Grandfather was already seated at the table. He smiled when he saw me.

"I thought maybe you ran away."

"I just went for a walk is all."

Mother put a baked dish with yellow squash, chicken, and sweet potatoes on the table. It was pretty brown on top, but not burned, and it smelled good.

"When I was your age, I ran away from home," said Grandfather as he used a big spoon to ladle out food onto all of our plates.

"Don't put ideas in his head," said my mother.

"Really?" It was hard to think of Grandfather as someone who had once been my age, let alone as a runaway. "Why did you do it?"

"I don't remember. But it must have been important to me at the time," said Grandfather.

"What happened?"

"I was never seen again," he said with a smile.

That made me smile too.

"Tell him what really happened," said my mother.

"I met a coyote and he convinced me to go home."

"No way," I said, smiling at him between bites of food.

He shook his head. He was not joking. "I sat out on a big hill at night and a coyote came out and howled at the moon. I listened to what he had to say about the night. It scared me so I went home."

"What was scary about it? I've heard coyotes howl most of my life, and it doesn't scare me."

Grandfather seemed thoughtful, as if he were recalling that day long ago when he was young. He was silent for a little while and then he said, "When his coyote voice was raised to the sky, it was like an invitation to me. Come and live as I live, said the coyote. You do not need your own kind. You have left them behind. Now you are a coyote. Come sit on this hill with me and howl at the moon!"

"I don't understand. I never heard a coyote sound like that," I said, wondering if the story was true.

"Maybe someday you will," said Grandfather. "There is much in the world to be heard, if ears want to listen. I was lucky that day. When the coyote asked me to leave my people behind and become like him, my heart would not let me. I went home because I wanted to be who I was, even if I was unhappy."

"Look. I didn't run away. I just went for a walk. I didn't mean for anybody to get upset!" I was getting tired of explaining.

"Eat, you two. We can talk later. This food has had enough hot air passing over it already," said my mother with a smile.

I ate everything on my plate and had a second plate almost as full as the first one. I drank two glasses of apple juice, too.

As I helped clear away the dishes, I kept thinking about the coyote. Maybe someday I would listen to a coyote again and I'd see if I heard the same things my grandfather heard. He's pretty smart about a lot of things, so if he said he heard the coyote say all that, maybe he did.

My mother washed the dishes and my grandfather dried them. I sat at the kitchen table and just listened to them talk. While they worked, they talked about the pueblo, about the life we had all lived there.

From the way Grandfather talked, it was plain he

liked the life he knew in the pueblo better than life here. He said something I had never heard before. My mother asked him why he hadn't tried to go back to the pueblo when he couldn't work in high steel anymore.

"I don't really know," said Grandfather White-feather. "Perhaps it is because I chased some dreams, the kind that come from the city, so long that they are a part of me and I am a part of them. When I go back, I am not at peace. I married here in the city, raised my son here for at least half of his life. He was able to go back to the pueblo. He found a peace I do not know and he made a life there for you and the boy. But I am not happy here and I am not happy there. So I live as much as I can in both places."

"If my father found peace there, why are we here now?"

They stopped doing the dishes and turned to look at me.

"Grandfather said we are here because of something you promised my father," I told my mother.

She looked angrily at my grandfather. "What did you tell him?"

"Only that there was a promise. The boy wants answers. You'll have to tell him sometime."

"He's not old enough. He won't understand."

Grandfather shook his head. It was plain he did not agree.

"If he understands only a little bit of it, maybe it

would be easier for him to get along here. You can't just make him do this. He is a human being and he needs to know why things are being done."

"I won't discuss it. And I don't want you talking about it either!" She had a dark look on her face, as if she remembered some old anger. "I don't want you meddling in this."

Grandfather bunched up the towel he had been using to dry the dishes and threw it into the sink. There were still more dishes to dry, but he was quitting. He turned his back on her and limped out of the room, his back set straight and angry.

I didn't know why they were fighting or why my mother wouldn't tell me things. Grandfather Whitefeather wanted to. They had a secret, that was plain, and they were keeping it from me. I wanted to know what it was, especially since it seemed to have something to do with my father.

My mother went on washing the dishes. I would have liked to ask her about it again, hoping she would change her mind, but I could tell it was the wrong thing to do.

"You want me to help you finish drying the dishes?" I offered.

"No. I don't need any help," she said, not looking at me.

So I went up to my room. I had a lot of nothing to do and my room seemed like the best place to do it in. I sat by the window and listened to cars go by in the street. It was getting dark outside so I sat there and just waited for night to fall. I was thinking that when the moon came up and a coyote howled out there somewhere, which would be strange and wonderful because a city is no place for a coyote, maybe, just maybe, it would say something to me.

But then I probably couldn't even hear it over the sound of traffic.

Chapter ⚡ Fourteen

My mother got her second paycheck, after two weeks of dishwashing work.

"I think there is some extra money, so if you want to go with me, Jimmy, we could look for some small things for the house."

"New stuff?"

"Maybe good secondhand," she said. "My job doesn't pay all that much." She seemed happier now although she was tired all the time.

"Is work going better?"

She sighed. "I am learning the restaurant business a little bit at a time. I know all the menu items by name now. Sometimes I fill in for the waitresses when they go on breaks. I hope that someday I will move up to being a waitress and making more money for all of us."

She cashed her paycheck at the bank and counted the bills silently. Then she said, "There might even be some extra money just for you, in case you want something special for your room."

I did want something special for my room. I wanted a window that opened out onto the desert. But I knew she couldn't give me that.

Grandfather had gone to a doctor because his legs were bothering him, so my mother and I went shopping. We didn't go to regular places. Mother said the stores that sold new things wanted too much money, so we went to thrift shops and secondhand stores. She bought a secondhand chair, which we had a hard time getting into the trunk of Grandfather's old car.

I still had the four dollars the lady that felt sorry for me had given me. I meant to tell my mother about it but never got around to it.

Since I spent so much time in my room and didn't have any friends, I bought a yo-yo. It was made of plastic but it was all dented and scuffed up and the string was full of knots, so it only cost a dime. I had seen one once but never had tried one. I bought a small paperback book that was a guidebook to reptiles and amphibians. It had lots of pictures of frogs and snakes and looked pretty interesting. For fifty cents I also bought a big glass storage jar that had a wooden lid. It was the kind of jar they used to have on the front counter of the trading post for penny candy.

I thought maybe I could catch a lizard, or maybe

a small garden snake, and keep him in it. I could put rocks and sand in the bottom, then some twigs. I knew I could catch insects, flies and crickets and such, so feeding a snake or lizard wouldn't be a problem. Of course, I didn't know if I could find reptiles here in the city, but just looking for one would help fill my time.

It wasn't that I was longing to have a pet, but I thought a jar with a lizard or snake in it would remind me of the desert.

Mother was busy looking at clothes, holding up blouses she thought might fit against her chest. So I just went up front and paid for my stuff with my own money and took it outside and put it on the back seat of the car. I still had quite a bit of money left.

With the chair in the trunk and the stuff I bought, I felt it was a pretty good day. I hadn't had a lot of good days since we had come here, so I was feeling a little better than usual.

My mother came out with some clothes, a pocketbook, and a plastic bag. She opened the car door and handed me the bag. "I got something for you," she said, and she got in and started the car.

I held the bag, feeling guilty because it seemed as if I had got a lot of things for me already without her giving me something, too.

Mother stopped for a stoplight. "Go on. Open the bag. I think you'll like it."

I opened the bag and stuck my hand inside. It was a pair of shoes my size with wheels on them.

"Do you like them?"

"What are they?"

"Roller skates. Don't you know about roller skates?" My mother sighed. "I had a pair when I was your age. Only they weren't this fancy. They had small, metal wheels, not nice rubber like these, and they had to be buckled onto your shoes or boots."

"I've seen kids in the neighborhood using them, but I didn't know what they were called." It was one of the best gifts anybody had ever given me. I didn't know what I'd done to be worthy of it. I had watched the kids using them with envy and had wished for a pair of skates, too, even though I didn't know the name for them. When the kids went skating down the street, it was as if they had a car under their shoes.

"I can teach you how to use them. Then you can skate up and down the sidewalk on our street. Maybe you can skate with the other kids. It will take practice, but I remember how fun it can be. Do you like them?" She seemed eager to have me like the skates. I thought they were great.

If I had known she was going to spend so much on me, I would have bought her and Grandfather something instead of spending so much on myself.

"I like them, but you might want me to take them back," I said, figuring now I was going to have to show her what I bought. I remembered what my father said about having too many things.

Mother frowned. She thought I was ungrateful.

We reached the street our house was on and Mother pulled up into the driveway and shut the engine off. She turned and looked at me and sighed.

"Don't you want them?"

I turned in the seat and got the yo-yo, the book, and the jar and lifted them into the front seat.

"I already got this stuff for me. Father would say I have too many things all at once. So maybe some of this will have to go back."

She was shocked. And then she was furious. I had never seen her so mad. "I can't believe it! We didn't raise you like that! Jimmy! I just can't believe you'd steal those things! I'm glad your father wasn't alive to see this!"

"Wait a minute. I didn't—"

"We're going to take them back!" She started the car up and put it in reverse. We pulled out into the street with a sudden jerk and the car tires squealed. She kept her eyes straight ahead. "You're going to apologize for stealing these things, and if they don't put you in jail, then you and I are going to have a very long and very serious talk!"

"I bought those things. I had money! If you let me explain about the lady with—"

But she cut me off. She was in no mood to listen to anything I had to say. "Jimmy. Don't talk to me! Don't make it any worse. Don't you dare lie to me! You've fought me on everything since the first day we came here. You mark my words, from this day on, all of this is going to stop! I've had all I can take!"

A stoplight turned red and Mother hit the brakes hard. The glass jar slipped out of my hands and fell to the floor. It didn't break. I picked it up and was trying to figure out some way to get her to listen to me, but her mind was already made up.

"Why, Jimmy? Why? You've never done anything like this before!" She was almost crying.

Stealing is a very serious thing. It's one of the worst crimes, if not the worst, anyone in the pueblo can commit. I was getting angry right back at her. She wasn't listening to me, and she was saying I was a thief and a liar. I hate grown-ups when they think they know it all.

Mother parked the car in front of the store.

"Get your things and follow me. You pick up everything you stole. And I mean everything!" She was already out of the car, standing there on the sidewalk, giving me this cold, almost hateful stare. She had the roller skates in her hands.

"I'm taking these back too, Jimmy. A thief doesn't deserve presents!" she said. "We did not raise you to live this way. I am ashamed."

"I didn't steal anything!"

She turned her back on me and walked into the store. There was nothing I could do but follow her. The same woman who ran the cash register before was there waiting on a customer. She rang up the amount, thanked the woman for shopping there, and then looked at my mother and me. Seeing the troubled look on my mother's face, she asked, "What's the problem?"

82

"We have come to apologize and to return the things my son has stolen!" My mother took the book, yo-yo, and jar from my hands and put them on the counter top. The woman looked down at them and then looked at me.

I didn't know what to do. I shrugged and smiled at her, hoping that she remembered me from before.

"There must be some mistake," said the woman.

"There is no mistake," insisted my mother. "And I want to return these skates."

"That's your son?"

"Why, yes," said my mother, surprised at the question.

The woman leaned over the counter and winked at me. "When you bought this, you asked me if fifty cents was a good price for this jar. I said it was fair if you wanted the jar. You said you wanted it to put a lizard or a snake in it. I remembered that right, didn't I?"

I nodded. My mother looked as though somebody had hit her.

"Well, I'm glad you came back," said the woman. "I was thinking about that jar. If it is only going to be used as a home for a lizard or a snake, then probably fifty cents is too much money." She hit a button on the cash register and the drawer popped open. She got out a quarter and handed it to me.

"We'll make it twenty-five cents. Does that seem fair now?"

"It sounds very fair," I said. "And thank you for remembering me."

The woman looked at my mother. My mother looked as though she was having maybe the worst day of her entire life. She stared down at the floor and I knew she was about to cry.

"I am not a thief and I am not a liar. It makes me angry if somebody thinks bad things about me that are not true." I talked to them both, wanting them to know everything. "I went for a walk. A woman gave me four dollars because she said I was poor. I didn't want the money but she insisted that I take it. I still have some of it."

"I am sorry," said my mother. "I am so terribly sorry!"

"Do you still want to return the skates?" the woman asked. I could tell she felt bad for my mother.

Mother's shoulders started to shake and the tears began to flow and she ran out the door. She leaned against the car and cried.

"Everybody makes mistakes. Even mothers," said the woman. "God knows I made enough in my time with my own kids. Here, you take your things and your skates and run along. She's just made a mistake. It's hard to be right all the time. Try to make it easy for her because she's having a bad day."

That woman at the cash register was the first really kind person I had met in the city.

I went outside and put everything in the car. I took my mother by the hand and led her to the car door and opened it for her. She was still crying.

"Let's go home, Mother. Maybe later you can

teach me how to roller skate?" She nodded and I guess she knew I was trying to make it better. She tried to smile, but it didn't work so well.

She cried all the way home. Some days just seem to go that way. There is nothing anybody can do about it.

Chapter ✌ Fifteen

I spent most of Sunday morning falling down. Sometimes I fell over forward and sometimes I fell over backward. Roller skating is not something you just get up and do right away. First you have to hurt yourself a lot. And then hurt yourself some more. Then you can maybe stand up on roller skates.

I watched the other kids. They just went zooming by. They seemed to have been born on roller skates.

Maybe my legs are too long, I thought. Or maybe they are not long enough. I took the skates off and put my boots back on. I'd had enough fun for one day. I think I had bruises on some of my bruises.

My grandfather came out and watched me for a while, but he said it was too exciting. Life moved fast enough without trying to put wheels on shoes. He was laughing a lot when he said it.

My mother got up extra early that morning. Since it was Sunday, she had the day off. She had been kind of weepy all night, and I tried to stay away from her because I knew she felt bad, and I didn't want to remind her. I just hoped she would forget the whole thing.

She left in the car after a whispered conversation with Grandfather. I think he was giving her directions, because he was gesturing with his hands, left, then right, then left, as if showing her the way to get somewhere.

I put the skates on the porch and went up to my room. I put a bandage on my nose where it had tried to see how hard the concrete was. The concrete was a lot harder than my nose. I wanted to get something to drink and then go out and look for a lizard.

Practically the first thing I noticed when I got upstairs was that my glass jar was gone. I went downstairs and asked Grandfather if he had seen it.

He grinned and shook his head no, but he didn't fool me. He had seen it or at least knew where it was. Everybody seemed to have a secret these days.

I read my book on reptiles for a while up in my room. Then I heard Grandfather's old car pulling into the driveway, so I drifted downstairs to see what we were going to do for lunch. Falling down a lot can make you real hungry.

My mother and grandfather were standing in front of the kitchen table.

"Hey!" I said. "You're back. Have you seen my glass jar, and what's for lunch?"

They moved aside and I saw my glass jar sitting in the center of the table. There was sand on the bottom, and shiny black rocks like the kind from the high mesas. A short tree branch with the leaves trimmed off ran through the center of the jar. On the branch, looking like something carved out of turquoise, sat a tiny blue lizard.

"It's called a blue-tailed skink," said my mother. "It is my apology to you for not treating you like a human being, for forgetting who you are."

"It's the best apology anybody ever made," I said. I had never seen a lizard like that before. It was so blue it looked like it would glow in the dark.

"Do you forgive me?" she asked. Her voice trembled, and I hoped she wasn't going to cry again.

"I forgave you yesterday," I said. "And when I forgive somebody, they stay forgiven."

"I'll fix something for us all to eat then," said Grandfather. "I guess we can leave the lizard right where he is. We can look at him while we eat and think we are back in the desert." He started opening cupboards and taking out pots and pans. He seemed unusually cheerful.

"I'll talk with Jimmy until lunch is ready." Mother straightened her shoulders as she always does when she has to do something difficult.

Grandfather looked happy, as if something he had long hoped for was about to arrive.

"Let's go out and sit in the grass. I want to be out-doors to say the things I have to say. There are some things you can only bear to talk about when the sun is shining." She opened the door for me and we went outside together.

"Are you going to tell me the big secret?" I was curious why one day she wouldn't even consider telling me, but today, suddenly, she wanted me to know. It is hard sometimes to figure grown-ups out. They keep changing the rules all the time, just to suit them.

"Yesterday I realized you were a lot more grown-up than I thought you were. And in the same way, when I didn't listen to you, when I didn't think about how you felt, I was wrong. I was thinking too much about myself and not enough about you."

"What made you change your mind, I mean, about wanting to tell me?"

"Last night your grandfather said something to me about your father's death that woke me up. He said his death did not happen just to him and me, it happened to you, too, and it was time I thought of that."

"You don't have to explain things to me if it will make you feel bad," I said.

"I do feel bad, but I will feel worse if I don't tell you. There's a reason why we are here. It concerns you, it is about you, and you need to know what that reason is."

I sat in the grass and chewed on a grass stem.

The sun felt good on my back. If I closed my eyes, I could almost imagine I was back in the pueblo.

"It is our way to talk openly about the facts of life. So I know you will not be embarrassed by this story."

"So tell me about the promise," I said.

"Not yet. You have to know some other things first. It goes back to when I was pregnant with you."

I was surprised but I let her go on.

"My time was very near. It was a difficult pregnancy. I was sick that spring and had several high fevers and I was afraid that it had affected you."

"Wait. This is before I was even born?"

"About two months before you were supposed to come along," she said, smiling as if she remembered me from that time. "And I was as big as a horse and could barely walk. You were a big baby."

I smiled. "Go on."

"It was a long trip to the hospital. Your father was away working and planned to be back in time. But sometimes you can't plan things like babies. I started for the hospital in Flagstaff. Your grandfather had the same car he has now, and he drove me. I think he hit every pothole between the pueblo and Flagstaff. It was a special hospital, the only place that would take Indian women at the time. And the government paid for almost everything if you didn't have any money. We had almost nothing, and because of the fever I was afraid to try to have you at home. I wanted you born in the hospital in case there was trouble."

"Was there trouble?"

"Yes," she said, and she looked angry and sad. "But the trouble was not about you." She winced as if each word she said was somehow painful. "I went into labor long before your father could get there. I was lucky even to make it to the hospital on time."

She stopped talking and looked down at her hands. She clenched them and looked sad and seemed suddenly to be very, very far away.

"Then what?"

"Then the bad thing happened." She said it so quietly and in such a strange voice that it was almost scary.

"I was in a great deal of pain. I did not know there could be so much pain. A doctor came in with some forms for me to sign. I asked him what they meant. I was not educated. He used big words and talked fast. All I knew was I hurt. And I was scared. He made it sound like if I did not sign that paper, I couldn't have my baby in that hospital. I was so afraid for you, I would have signed anything!" She seemed to hate this memory, this doctor with the paper.

"A nurse came in to give me a shot for the pain. I wanted the shot so badly, but the doctor wouldn't let me have it until I signed the paper. So I signed it, but I did not read it. I asked for a copy to give to my husband, but they would not give it to me. That was when I knew it was wrong to sign, but I was too sick to stand up for myself." She sighed and her voice trembled with hurt. "How I wished your father could have been there!" A tear began in the corner of one eye and rolled slowly down her cheek. She brushed it away angrily.

"What was on the paper?"

"Let me tell it my way," she said. She seemed to choose her next words carefully.

"I gave birth, and you were the most beautiful baby in the world. I held you on my stomach, and I loved you!" She had a sudden look of joy on her face that made her look somehow younger. She reached for my hand. I felt embarrassed, but glad for her touch. She held on tightly.

"Then they took you away and said I would see you later that afternoon."

I was wondering about the paper. I was bursting to ask about it.

"That same afternoon, instead of bringing you in to see me, they wheeled me into an operating room. They gave me a shot. I was groggy and could not think straight. I tried to find out what was wrong, but the doctor said it was just routine, just to sleep, not to worry, they'd take care of everything."

"Were you sick? I mean from having me?"

"No. I had a normal delivery, a wonderful little baby boy, perfect in every way, with all his toes and fingers and no complications. I did not need an operation. But they gave me one anyway. It happened because of the paper I had signed."

"I don't understand. What happened?"

She let go of my hand and wiped tears from the corners of her eyes. She straightened her shoulders before she spoke again. "They gave me an operation that fixed it so I could never have any more children. You were to be the first and last child I would ever have. No brothers or sisters for you."

"But why would they do that?"

"Because I had signed a paper that said I wanted them to do it, even though I didn't know what the paper said. They tricked me into signing it."

"But why did they do that?"

"Because the government did not want any more Indian babies born. Because we were undesirable, or our skin was the wrong color, or we did not vote the right way, or because we cost the taxpayers money. It was never explained to me but it does not matter why. It only matters that it was their official policy!" Her voice shook now with anger and she balled her hands into fists.

"That stinks! That really stinks!" I was angry for her and sorry for us both. I would have liked having brothers or sisters.

"This did not just happen to me. It happened to many women. You must understand this is something that happened to us because we were Indian. Never forget that! Remember always, too, that they did this to us when we were afraid for the babies we were about to bring into this world. They used our fear against us. It is shameful that they would treat human beings that way. I do not want you to ever forget this."

"I hate white people!" I said. I didn't know any of them very well, but I had heard enough.

"No. Hating people is wrong. Do not let me hear you say that ever. But you can hate the bad things they do."

"Okay, I won't say it, but it's not fair. This should never have happened!"

"No, it should never have happened, but it did." She unclenched her fists and made a gesture of throwing something away. She meant it was over and done with.

"Did you want more children?"

"Oh yes. We did not want you to make your journey through this life alone. We wanted a house full of children because such a house is full of life."

"I am sorry." I felt so bad for her.

"It is a sorrow that will never go away. A child should have brothers and sisters to grow up with and grow old with," she said, and she squeezed my hand. "And because of that, I made a promise to your father."

At last, the secret she had been keeping from me!

"If we know only our own world, we will always be victims. What we do not understand will always be used against us," she said. "Your father was angry all his life that he could not protect me, that he could not save me from what happened, that I was not able to defend myself."

I started to speak, but she motioned me to be silent.

"Let me finish. Your father wanted you to be educated. Not because he did not want you to live in the pueblo, not because he did not want you to learn what our way of life has to teach. But because in this time we need brave defenders who can live in and understand both worlds!" My mother's voice rose with anger and remembrance.

"But I would rather live in the pueblo. When you tell me things like this, the whole rest of the world seems even more rotten. So why would he want me to be where we are?"

"Because you must be the defender of the brothers and sisters you never had! You must be their voice! We are not going to stay here forever. When you are wise enough to understand the city, to understand the way this world works, when you know how to defend us against all the lies and treacheries and untruths, when you know enough about what is here for us that is worth having and can share that and throw out the bad, then we can all go home."

"I thought this was supposed to be our new home."

"This place can never be home. Your grandfather lives here because he is tainted by too much of the things he has found here. He cannot be happy back in our world, but we do not hope to be happy here. The city is a place to learn, to gather things we can take back with us to protect our true home."

"I'm glad you told me," I said, although it was so

much to think about all at once that I didn't really know. This seemed like the biggest thing in the world to ask of someone as young as me. I was just a kid, after all.

"Does knowing this make you happier now, about being here? Knowing that it is not meant to be forever?"

"No." I was sure about that.

"I intend to keep my promise to your father," said my mother, and her voice was calm and steady and determined. "We have put all our trust in you for tomorrow."

"And that's the reason why we are here? Because of that promise?"

"That's right," she said softly. "Other things, too, but mostly this. Is it all clear now to you?"

"Now I understand," I said. I'd heard more than I wanted to know.

"But do you? Do you really know why? I can say what I say and do what I do because my heart has become a stone that keeps its promise. Nothing can move me from this, even though I hate it here, too!"

I felt even more confused and tried to see it the way she did. I could guess why she felt like this, and probably I should feel the same way because I loved Father as much as she did. But even though I now knew what they wanted of me, it did not help much. Everything they asked was nothing but a big ache and a hardship. I felt crushed under the weight of their hopes.

I could almost hear my father talking to me. The promise was something he would want me to keep. But it all seemed so unclear. How could I miss brothers and sisters I never had? And then leave everything I loved behind, just to be their voice? It was just too confusing, and I did not feel worthy. I felt so blue then, so sad about the way life seemed to be, that I wanted the ground to open up and swallow me.

"I do it for the children I could not have. For all the babies yet to be born," she said. "So that it will never happen again."

I knew the promise was something I was supposed to keep, too, for our brothers and sisters yet to be. Such promises are sacred.

They asked too much of someone so small.

Grandfather called us in to eat. We sat and stared at our food. Nobody seemed to be hungry or to feel like talking. Only Grandfather seemed to understand what to say. He looked at us both and said, "Once there was a great chief of our pueblo. He was a man who saw far into the future, and he made great promises for our children and our children's children."

We both stared at him as if he had the answer to something.

"At the end of his life, no chief had ever been so greatly honored by his people, yet all of his days were full of strife and trouble. This is what he said about life, about living up to promises."

Mother was almost in tears. There was even a catch in Grandfather's voice. I knew everything I had heard today was something they had been carrying with them that still hurt as much now as when it happened all those years ago.

"The chief said, 'When you try to live up to a promise, to live up to something bigger than life itself, life makes you feel small under the weight.'"

I knew how that was. The things they wanted me to do made me feel smaller than the little lizard in the jar, who stared at me quietly, dreaming of whatever it is that lizards dream of.

"'Each year, the weight of those promises gets heavier, and the river gets deeper and harder to cross.'" Grandfather put his hand on the glass jar and the lizard inside jumped off the branch, forgetting his dream. He crouched down in fright at the bottom of the jar.

"'But a man who carries it becomes a giant,'" finished Grandfather.

I hoped he was right.

Chapter ❧ Sixteen

"I used to dream that I would wake up one day and find all of us back in the pueblo," I said at breakfast a few days later. I ate a bite of corncake. My mother, across the kitchen table, watched me unhappily.

"And I dream I will wake up one day and a whole day will go by with no complaints," she said, putting another corncake on my plate.

"I don't have that dream anymore," I said, "and I am not really complaining. At least I don't mean to."

And I did mean that. Now that I understood the promise my mother made my father, I got through the days a little better. Not that I was happy. Being happy didn't seem to count much against the burden of keeping the promise. But I was a little more at ease.

"We've been in the city only six weeks. You have to give it some more time," she said.

Those six weeks seemed more like six years, but I didn't say so aloud.

"Summer is almost over and soon you'll start school. Then you will find better things to fill your days," she said.

I wasn't looking forward to it. I knew this was what my father wanted for me, but it was hard for me to want it, too. I wasn't afraid of school. That wasn't the problem. We had a schoolteacher back at the pueblo. I learned to read and write and do some math, but my mother said this was too limited. Still, I read most of the books I could find or borrow. Books cost too much, except maybe secondhand, so nobody in the pueblo had very many. So it wasn't like I was stupid and couldn't read or something like that.

"It was your father's dream and now it is ours. Try to remember that."

"I won't forget. You don't let me. You only remind me about every day or so!" I wasn't angry at her, just tired of being constantly reminded of something I already knew.

She didn't take the hint.

"School in the city is not about a better life. It is about living a smarter life when we go back home. Try to think of it that way," she said.

Her saying it didn't make it so. I didn't quite believe her, I still missed my father, and I felt bad about being where we were. But there was no use telling her any of that.

"You shouldn't be so gloomy. Already you know your way around the neighborhood. And before long you will make friends here, too, I know it."

I didn't tell her I'd already met some kids my age on this street, but they didn't seem friendly. It seemed as though I didn't know how to talk to them and they didn't want to talk to me. I pushed my corncake around on my plate.

"Your grandfather and I both expect you to make friends here. It will show us that you are doing your best to fit in."

"I don't need friends. My friends are back in the pueblo. I don't need any here."

My mother shook her head disapprovingly.

If I made friends, I'd do it for me, not to prove that I was trying to fit in. I wished they could understand that! There were times I wished I had a friend, not just to get them off my back but because I was getting lonely for my friends back at the pueblo.

It was getting so I hated going back to the house. My mother was sure to ask me who I played with, and since the answer was no one she always acted very disappointed. She always seemed to think it was my fault.

My mother got up from the table. It was time for her to leave for work.

"Don't go too far from the house this morning. And make an effort to meet some of the kids on this street. Will you promise me you will try?"

I nodded yes. Grown-ups can really bug you. They get on a subject and never get off it.

I had already decided that today was the day. I was going to get my skates and go outside as soon as she was gone. I was determined to make friends with the first kid I saw even if I had to rope one.

Which is how I got the black eye.

I put my skates on. I was learning how to use them. I still fell a lot but could move down the sidewalk fairly well. Moving was one thing. Stopping was something else. Sometimes falling down was the only way I could stop.

I still felt pretty shaky. I got down to the corner and only fell twice. When I turned the corner, somebody was coming the other way on skates.

The skater was pretty fast and heading right for me, so I tried to turn and move out of the way, but my legs got tangled. I stumbled backward.

The other skater waved her arms wildly, like a bird that can't remember how to fly, then plowed right into me, knocking me down. I groaned under her weight and turned sideways until she rolled off me.

"Hey! Why don't you watch where you're going!" I said. I sat up slowly, staring at a scrape on my elbow.

The girl was probably my age, or a little older. "I *was* watching. That's how come I hit you!" She smiled at me. "Are you hurt?"

"I don't think I need a medicine man," I said, though my elbow hurt.

"I've seen you around the neighborhood. I guess you're an Indian, huh?"

I didn't say yes or no to that. I'd let her figure it out.

"I've seen the old Indian who lives in the house you're staying in. That's why I asked. You look like him."

"He's my grandfather," I admitted.

"My name is Claire. I live farther down on Clayton. I've seen you skate by my house."

We got up slowly. Getting up is hard with skates on. I think I'd fallen down almost as many times just trying to get back up as I had actually skating. She was just about as shaky as I was.

"I'm glad to see somebody else is as bad at skating as I am," she said. We were both waving our arms in circles, trying to keep our balance. She grabbed my arm to steady herself. It pulled me just enough off balance that I felt my skates going out from under me. I fell forward, and she came crashing down on top of me again.

I hurt my other elbow and I was going to be mad about it. After all, it was Claire's fault. She rolled off me and I was going to say something nasty, but she was smiling at me and pointing at a big scrape on each of her elbows.

"Four elbows! Four scrapes!" She laughed. "Now that's what I call skating!"

I started to laugh, too, in spite of the pain.

"At least we are equally embarrassing," said Claire.

"I would say we don't have enough skates," I suggested.

"What do you mean?"

"We need one skate for each elbow, too, since they seem to be on the ground almost as much as our feet," I said.

And we started laughing all over again.

Later we found that by linking our arms together, we could skate slowly side by side down the sidewalk. By leaning against each other, we seemed to get around the problem of leaning too far forward or too far back, which is what caused most of our spills.

Claire was funny. She said things that were all mixed up and kept making me laugh. Sometimes she talked about things I knew nothing about, but we got along pretty well. I didn't say it aloud, but it felt like I had made a friend after all.

We hit a fairly straight stretch of sidewalk so we decided to be fearless and speeded up. It was the fastest I had ever gone on skates. We were pretty much zipping right along when the trouble started.

Two big white men got out of a big car parked along the curb. They started to cross the sidewalk.

"Hey, watch out!" Claire cried.

The men stepped back as we came roaring down on them. We coasted, trying to slow down. We were going to miss them.

We were almost past them when one man laughed and stuck his foot out in front of Claire, tripping her. Her arm pulled out of mine and she fell forward onto the sidewalk with a big bang. I waved my arms wildly, teetered sideways, ended up on one skate, and couldn't get the other one back under me. I went crashing off the sidewalk at an angle. A thick tree branch smashed into my face. It stung, but didn't stop me. I kept going until a big bush on somebody's lawn broke my fall. That made it easy on me but hard on the bush.

The two men laughed and crossed the sidewalk. The man who had tripped Claire said, "The nigger fell down and went boom!" They opened the door of a house and went inside.

I was up and angry. I tried to run back to Claire, but it wasn't possible with the skates on.

Claire had hurt her knee. She had hit the pavement pretty hard, hard enough to make anyone cry. I got my skates off as quick as I could and ran barefoot to her. She was holding her knee and rocking back and forth.

"I'm gonna knock on their door and when they come out, I'll brain them with my skates!" I yelled.

"Don't waste your time on them," she said, and I saw she wasn't crying. "I'm gonna be fine."

"But they hurt you!"

"They think they did a lot but they only hurt me a little."

"Aren't you angry at them? For what they did to you?"

"Sure! But it wouldn't change them. If they're so stupid they get a kick out of knocking down kids because they don't like the color of their skin, then they're just too stupid to even deal with!"

"I could take my skates and really mess up the

windshield of their car! Then maybe next time they'd think twice about—"

"No way. You do that and they've won. They've made you sink to their own level," she said, her voice ringing with conviction.

"Yeah, but if you want justice, then you have to fight fire with fire," I began.

She cut me off again. "No. We're smarter than that. If you bust up their car, they just get angry and they don't learn anything. They are stupid and they'll be stupid tomorrow and nothing you or I do will change that. When it comes to racism the only way you win is you get smarter than they are, and you stay smarter!"

It would not have been my father's way of doing things, but it appealed to me. I didn't know how she figured it that way. It seemed they had won and we had lost. But Claire didn't act like somebody who was defeated. That confused me. She skinned her elbow and laughed about it. She seemed to know how to act in a completely different way than I was used to. She reminded me of my grandfather, the way she looked at things.

"He meant to hurt you, but you don't act like a victim," I said.

"He hurt me on the outside, but I'm not going to let him hurt me on the inside," she said. "Besides, my father always said never go to the wall for anything small."

"What does that mean?"

"Save yourself for the really big fights in life.

Don't waste your energy on the small stupidities!"
she said. "Help me get my skates off, will you? I
think I've had enough skating for one day."

I bent over and helped untie her skates, thinking
about what she said. I don't know how I would
have acted in her place. Probably if somebody had
tried to hit me, I would have hit him right back. I
knew she had some wisdom I did not have, sensed
it was something she had learned here in the city
that I must learn, too.

"Most people aren't like that," she said, meaning
the two white men. "You'll find lots of good people
here, too."

"I'm sorry you got hurt," I said. "But I like your
bravery."

I helped her to her feet. She was limping, but she
was able to walk.

"At least we were having fun. Guess I better head
for home and put some ice on my knee," she said.
"If you can wait until my knee is better, maybe we
could do some more skating together."

"I'd like that," I said, and I meant it. "One thing
still puzzles me though. What's a nigger?"

"You mean you don't know?" She seemed gen-
uinely surprised.

"It's a new word to me."

"It's what ignorant, stupid white people call black
people!" she said. "A pueblo must be a pretty good
place if you never heard that word. Someday you'll
have to tell me what it's like to grow up there."

"Sure!" I liked the idea and was sure there was a

lot she could tell me in return about living in the city.

I had made a friend! She limped off for home with a cheery wave. "Take care of that knee!" I called out after her.

"See ya soon!" she called back. Then she was gone.

I slung my skates over my shoulder and headed for home. My face was aching where it had hit the tree branch. I must have hit it harder than I realized, because by the time I got back to the house I had a pretty good start on a black eye.

But I didn't mind—I also had a pretty good start on a friend. One canceled the other one out.

Chapter ✦ Seventeen

Claire and I didn't skate together again. Probably we were both trying to be kind to our elbows.

But we did other things just as fun, and she introduced me to some of her friends.

It helped having someone my own age to talk to. But the good things that made good days were too few and too far between. There never seemed to be a good day like the good days at the pueblo.

My mother was pleased about Claire and her friends and even bugged me about inviting them over to the house. I thought I'd probably do that, not for her sake but for mine. It was good to have friends.

But there was too much missing for anything to really be a comfort. I thought about my father a lot, and missed him more in this place now than I ever did back in the pueblo. Back there, he still seemed to be in my world. But in the city, everything about him being gone just seemed worse somehow. Sometimes I felt like I was drowning in a river, weighed down by all the promises I couldn't keep. I just stumbled through the days, mostly wandering around the city looking at things.

What I saw made everything worse. Sometimes you see things that are so bad you just can't bear to talk about them.

I tried to cross the room without my grandfather seeing me, but his eyes were eagle sharp. He saw things nobody else could.

"Jimmy Whitefeather!" he called out, and I turned to face him.

"Jimmy. Tell me what you saw today, grandson, that makes you so unhappy," said Grandfather.

"What makes you think that?" I asked. But I knew he knew. You can't hide anything from Grandfather Whitefeather.

"There are many ways to walk into a room, grandson. Sometimes it is with joy and summer in your heart. But today you walk as if winter is at your back. Something must be wrong. Come sit with me."

We sat together on an old Navaho blanket on the floor. There were chairs in the room but Grandfather liked sitting on the floor best. He waited silently, respectfully, for me to answer his question.

I didn't want to, but he looked at me and I knew

I had to tell him. There was no escaping Grandfather.

"Today I saw a woman behind the supermarket. She was bent over and digging around in a garbage can with a stick."

The smile on Grandfather's face faded. "And why was she doing that, do you think?" he asked, but I think he already knew.

"I think she was hungry. I think she was looking for food."

"The city can be an unhappy place," said Grandfather.

"There was a little girl with her, not even big enough to be in school. She was thin and she looked tired. She looked sick!"

"And you feel bad, Jimmy," said Grandfather. "It means you have a caring heart. That is good. It means you have good feelings."

"If there's so much to learn here, if this is such a great place to get smarter," I protested, "why should mothers and children go hungry here?"

"I have lived a long time," said Grandfather. "I do not know why the world is the way it is. It is not the world I make for myself."

"If we had money, we could help them. We could give them food," I said.

"It is all we can do to feed ourselves," said Grandfather. "It is not easy. Your mother works hard to feed us all."

"If this was the pueblo, somebody would try to help them."

"Yes. But this is not the pueblo."

"I don't need to be reminded," I said.

"You can think of many reasons why you do not like it here in the city. But then so can I. Even your father had mixed feelings about this place," admitted Grandfather.

I nodded yes. "My father used to say a man can tell how tall he is by how far he sees. In the city, there are no open spaces. So to me the city seems big but all the people are small in it. I don't like it!"

"Your mother says you only have to live here until you finish school," Grandfather reminded me. "That is not a long time."

"Probably just a hundred years or forever, whichever is longer. Don't forget, she's talking about college, too. Maybe she wants me to be a doctor or something like that."

Maybe that was really the dream my father and mother had for me, that I would become a doctor and go back to the pueblo and help our children. But I was just a kid. It didn't seem fair that all the dreams had to depend on me.

Grandfather looked solemn. "Life isn't about what you or anyone else wants, it's about what you get."

That sounded like something really wise. I didn't like it and hoped it wasn't true, but it probably was. So I said, "When my father was alive, we lived in a real house and everything made sense and I thought life was going to go on like that forever. Maybe nothing is supposed to be forever."

"The wind blows first this way, and then it turns and nothing is ever the same again," said Grandfather. "That is both life's greatest sadness and its greatest joy. You remember how your house was the sunniest house in the whole pueblo and the sky was always with you. Those were happy times, but they do not last." He was right about that. Now the sky hides behind buildings and the land is buried in concrete.

I was nine when my father got sick. We spent all our money on hospitals and medicines. It didn't do any good. He just got thinner and sicker every day. Father did not live to see my tenth birthday.

Mother made him a promise, and here we were and here we would unhappily stay. Who was happy didn't seem to count much against keeping that promise. It seemed bigger than the whole world.

I didn't see how we could ever be happy again. Now Mother worked all day and was always tired. Sometimes at night, when she thought I didn't hear her, she cried alone in her room.

I wished Grandfather hadn't reminded me that this was not the pueblo. I went up to my room and gave my lizard a cricket I had caught. He kept running around and around in his jar, as if looking for a way out.

I felt the same way. I kept running around and around, but there was no way out.

Chapter ✿ Eighteen

I had too much to think about.

My father finished high school, but my mother only got as far as her junior year. She had to drop out because she was pregnant with me. She said she'd rather have me than a high school diploma any old day, but there had to be times when she wished she had both. She worked awful hard and got paid very little. Every month when the bills came, she got the blues and nothing I did or said seemed to cheer her up.

There was another reason we had to live in the city, besides the promise. Grandfather was a lot sicker than he let on, and he was alone in the world except for us.

Grandfather always had a fancy speech about why he lived in the city and not in the pueblo. But it wasn't exactly truthful. The truth was, he desperately wanted to go home, to live out the last of his days in the pueblo.

But he saw some special doctors in the city. He wasn't dying, but almost every week he had to have shots in his legs. He couldn't get those shots back in the pueblo so he was stuck here. Without the shots, walking became just too painful for him to bear. Besides, if he stayed in the city his accident insurance still paid for them.

I took care of him. Sometimes his legs ached and he couldn't walk so well. He tried to smile, but I knew he hurt all the time.

I came down to see what we were going to do about dinner. Mother was still at work. In fact, she was already late, and I was hungry. I was thinking about the woman and the little girl.

Grandfather seemed to know what I was thinking about.

"Forget about the world out there." Grandfather smiled at me. "The city is outside, but in here," his arms went wide and seemed to hug the whole room, "this is Indian country, blue skies and green growing grass. There is no city in here."

Grandfather turned his head and seemed to shade his eyes from the sun. He held himself like a man standing on a mountain, looking out over the valley below. I had seen him many times like this. He called it the time when the magic began.

Grandfather closed his eyes, and his voice traveled back to the time before we came here. "I see a day as bright as this day, in a summer of long ago. The pueblo walls shine with the glory of night rain. The gourds your father shaped into birdhouses are full of young birds, crying eagerly for food. Above the pueblo a many-colored rainbow dances across the sky. Are you with me, grandson, in this golden day?" asked Grandfather on the edge of the dream.

I was supposed to answer yes, but I didn't say anything. If he wanted to hide in the house and pretend, that was okay, but it wasn't for me.

"The rainbow!" cried Grandfather, excited. "Your father laughs to see such beauty above and your mother thinks it is not just a rainbow, but the bridge to another world."

He held out his hand to me, but I did not take it.

Grandfather stood in the room and in that long-ago summer day.

"I feel the sun-heated earth beneath my feet. The air smells of sage and the clean breath of the high mountains. What shall we do in the day of the rainbow? Shall we hunt the forest for the fearsome sight of some great beast, or fish the far stream for the great-grandfather of mountain trout?" Grandfather looked eager, as if his feet already moved him on the path of these adventures. He stood in a world of forest, mountain, and stream, a world full of days upon which it never rained without rainbows.

Standing in his living room, I could look through the front window and see the cars moving in rush-hour traffic. I saw a forest of ugly buildings and a stream of concrete streets, where little children went to bed hungry. I never saw any rainbows here.

Grandfather's voice almost pleaded with me.

"We make a world for ourselves!" He held out his hand to me again. "See how I shape it in my hands."

"I don't feel like pretending," I said. "Besides, it's all just talk."

"Where the heart walks, only truth comes, if you believe," said Grandfather gently. He opened his eyes and looked at me. He seemed suddenly sad. "I'll make the world and we'll go there."

He still held his hand out. But I didn't take it.

"Maybe I don't believe anymore," I said.

I thought about the little sick girl and the woman. They were real and Grandfather's world wasn't. When I turned to leave the room, I saw the hurt in Grandfather's eyes, but I left anyway.

Chapter ⚡ Nineteen

Mother finally came home, hours late.

She asked us to come into the living room because she had something important to tell us. Grandfather came out of his room slowly. Somehow today, maybe because I wouldn't dream with him, he looked very tired and older than I ever remembered him being. He went in and sat down quietly, keeping his head turned so he did not have to look at me.

"I hope you two haven't been fighting," said Mother, noticing our mood. "Because I have some bad news."

"We don't fight," said Grandfather. "Some days we are just different people. Are you ill, daughter?"

"Worse. I lost my job today."

"Oh," said Grandfather. And that was all he said.

"Why?" I asked.

"They didn't say why," she said, and she wrapped her arms around her chest as if in so much need of a hug she had to give herself one.

"I don't know how we are going to eat," she said. Her hands trembled, and I was afraid she was going to cry. "I spent a little bit more than I counted on this week."

Grandfather got up slowly, went to her, and put his arm around her.

"Tomorrow will come and you will do what tomorrow asks of you," he said. "I do not worry about it because you are strong and brave."

Mother smiled. "I found that job. I guess I can find another one."

"I see the walls of the pueblo shining in the sun," said Grandfather. "Come, let us journey there. Let us go home."

Mother sat down on the floor with Grandfather and turned to look at me. She wanted me to sit there with her. But I was angry.

"It would be good to go home," said Mother.

"Would you like a day with a rainbow?" asked Grandfather.

"No. I want a day with wind," said Mother. "The kind of wind that blows troubles away."

Grandfather closed his eyes. He shivered as if a sudden draft had passed over him. "I feel a wind so strong it opens all the doors of the houses."

Mother had her eyes closed too. "And the wind chases everybody outdoors. The squash gardens need to be weeded. The corn needs to be watered and my neighbors have happy secrets to share."

"Search the pueblo. Find your son's favorite fish spear," said Grandfather. "Jimmy is going fishing with his father, and his mother has to make them something sweet to eat. Fishing is hungry work."

"Jimmy, what kind of fish will you catch?" said Mother.

I did not want to see the world through Grandfather's eyes. "I'm busy. I have to go up to my room."

Mother opened her eyes, looked at me, and shook her head. "Show your grandfather respect. Come sit with us."

"*No!* It's stupid to do this. It doesn't change anything."

I meant what I said, but I could see the hurt look in Grandfather's eyes. I stayed put. I did not sit down with them.

My mother did not look at me. She spoke with her eyes closed. "When it gets bad, Jimmy, when it seems so bad I don't think I want to live, at those times I need to dream. I need to be in the life we lived and to be there with him and you. I know what's real, Jimmy. We all do, but dreams are the windows that make the human house livable."

"Dreams are just lies. They don't change anything. You can't eat them when you're hungry!" She hadn't seen the sick little girl, but I had.

Grandfather smiled sadly and said, "They change us. We are filled with dreams."

120

"I don't see any good to that."

"You will see the good one day," said Grandfather patiently. "Without dreams, how could we live here?"

I turned my back on them and went to my room, back to my glass jar.

Chapter ✦ Twenty

The next day nothing was different.

Mother got up early. She was all dressed up when she came into my room before I even got out of bed.

"Will you help take care of Grandfather for me today?" she said.

"Where are you going?" I asked.

"To look for a job," she said. Her hands were shaking when she put her coffee cup down on the orange crate next to my bed. I thought she was really scared and it made me feel sick inside.

"Some day all of this will seem worthwhile. The bad times will just make us all stronger," she said. But it was plain she was the one who needed to be cheered up. I knew I was supposed to say something, but I didn't feel like it. We sat there for a while without speaking.

Finally she smiled at me and got up to go. "Look

in on your grandfather. See how he's feeling. If he's up to it, you can help him go out on an errand. I gave him some money to buy groceries. It's just about all the money we have. You can help him carry the food back from the store in his wagon. But if he's not up to it, we can go in the car later."

I thought about the woman and the sick little girl looking for food in the garbage. It was something I wanted to talk about because it made me feel helpless, but I knew she had too much on her mind already.

I just wanted to get far away from the house and Grandfather and his dreams. I wanted to tell her I was too busy to help, but I knew it would make her cry. I didn't say anything.

She left then, and I heard her walk through the kitchen and out the back door. I waited until I heard the car start before I got up and put my jeans and boots on. I also put on the ribbon shirt my mother gave me during a green corn dance. I used to wear it when I had things to be happy about.

When I still knew how to be happy.

I started to sneak out of the house, thinking that Grandfather could take care of himself. He was just too old to understand the world. In my eyes, the city was ugly and dirty. All the bad things I saw here were real. I was trapped like a lizard in a glass jar, dreaming of a desert that I might never see again.

The city was not the world my grandfather dreamed about. If they were going to make me stay here, I wasn't going to dream about everything I'd lost.

I was out the back door, across the yard, and almost into the street before I realized I wasn't alone. Grandfather was crouched down in the dirt at the end of the driveway, staring at a handful of grass he had plucked.

"Good to see you up so early," he said, getting up slowly. I could tell his legs hurt him today. "C'mon, we have work to do. Get my bring-'em-back wagon."

I shrugged. Guess I had no choice but to go along with him. I hauled the old, red wagon out of the shed. One of the wheels was warped, but the wagon still pulled well enough to carry groceries in.

Grandfather and I started out for the supermarket. Six weeks ago I thought a supermarket was pretty amazing. Now it was just another boring place to go. As usual, we took the shortcut through the alley behind the store. We went past the bin where they keep the cardboard boxes and the garbage cans.

The woman with the little girl was poking around in one of the garbage cans again with a stick. She speared a rotten head of lettuce and brought it out.

"Look, Grandfather, look!" I said.

The little girl was at her mother's feet, holding on to her dress. She was very thin and pale, and her dress was torn. She looked very tired and sad.

Grandfather turned and saw the woman and the girl. He had a strange, angry look on his face.

The little girl coughed weakly.

I wanted to stop and go over to them, but Grandfather took my arm and pulled me along.

"Don't stare at them," said Grandfather in a whisper. The woman was looking at us. She put her arms around the moldy lettuce as if to protect it.

"But, Grandfather," I began. His hand on my arm tightened suddenly, and he marched me past them. We went around the end of the building and couldn't see the woman and the child anymore.

"You can't just pretend they aren't there, Grandfather!" I said angrily.

"If you stare at them, you'll embarrass them," said Grandfather calmly, as if nothing bothered him.

"Why didn't we stop and talk to them?" I wanted to know. "We could have told them we were sorry."

"What good would that have done?" asked Grandfather. "They can't eat words."

"Maybe you can dream them up some frybread," I said, feeling mean but not knowing why. "If we're going to pretend we can't see them, maybe we can pretend they are full of food, too."

He stopped walking and looked at me. "I did not know you were so upset."

I shrugged. "I'm tough. I can take it."

"No. You do not have to take it." He looked thoughtful and began to walk again. He did not look at me. "You think about the mother and her hungry little girl and you feel hopeless. Perhaps it seems like the promise we ask you to keep. You want to do something, to do what is right, but you do not have the means to do it. Is that just about how you feel?"

I didn't have any answer to that, but it was close to how I felt. Even if I had an answer, I wouldn't tell him. Let him pretend I was answering him. I tugged on the wagon handle, got the wagon back in motion, and followed him.

When we reached the front door of the store, Grandfather said something I didn't understand. "Sometimes it is only the small heart that sees and knows the truth and shames a heart that has almost forgotten who he is." The door opened automatically and we went into the store.

Grandfather had his money in his hand and he motioned me toward the first aisle. I pulled the wagon along behind. I couldn't forget how I felt. "I don't see the harm in telling them why we are sorry for them. It's a little more honest than trying to dream something is something when it isn't!" Let him answer that one.

"Why should we be sorry? We have done nothing wrong," said Grandfather.

"You are a stupid old man and you make me sick!" I said.

Grandfather stopped and looked at me. He was smiling, not angry like I thought he would be. I was sorry I said it, but Grandfather didn't seem to mind.

"If you could see the world through my eyes, if you could feel the world I shape with my hands,

126

you would understand," he said, and tried to put his hand on my shoulder. I moved away and wouldn't let him touch me. And I could tell that that hurt his feelings.

He came up and took the wagon handle out of my hands.

"Wait outside for me. I'll pick up what we need and meet you in the parking lot."

I tried to take the handle back, but he was too strong for me.

"Mother says I have to help," I said.

He gave me a very stern look, so I shrugged and went outside. I sat down on the curb and waited for him to come out.

I waited for what seemed like forever before the door opened and Grandfather came out with the wagon. It was really loaded.

"I'm sorry," said Grandfather. "I spent all the money. I was hoping there would be enough left to buy you some candy."

"I don't want any candy," I said. "If you bought me some, I'd give it away."

"Yes, I know," said Grandfather.

I took the handle of the wagon from him and I could tell by the way he walked that he was glad I was going to pull the wagon now. His legs must have really hurt. His knees were stiff and he hardly moved his feet when he walked. I walked slow so he could keep up. We went around the end of the building and turned into the alley.

The woman was still there. Behind her was an old, rusty shopping cart with clothes and some broken toys in it. She was sitting on the ground next to the little girl. She had a small pile of moldy lettuce and broken carrots in her lap. She was trying to brush the dirt off them.

The little girl looked up at us as we walked by. I turned my head so I wouldn't have to look at her. I knew my grandfather wouldn't let me do anything for them.

There was a sudden jerk, and the weight of the wagon I was pulling changed. I stopped. Grandfather was taking the bags out of the wagon and setting them down in the alley near the woman.

He did not look at her. He emptied the wagon, almost falling when he put the last bag on the ground.

I just stood there staring as Grandfather tilted the bags and gently emptied them. Big cans of baby formula and small jars of baby food spilled out all over the alley. There was a small box of animal crackers. There were jars of already-made oatmeal and little plastic bottles of fruit juice. There was a gallon of milk and a large bag of cookies.

"You don't have to do that," the woman said. She spoke real loud, as if she were almost angry.

Grandfather did not look at her.

"Had an accident," he said, acting as if he spoke to somebody who wasn't even there. "The wagon overturned and all our groceries spilled out. We didn't notice it until we got home, so whoever finds our groceries is very lucky. The world has smiled on them."

The woman got up slowly and started toward the pile of food. She seemed afraid.

Grandfather put the empty sacks back in the wagon, standing them up neatly as if they were still full. He put his hand over mine on the handle of the wagon and began to move slowly, pulling the empty wagon behind us.

The little girl ran to the pile of groceries and seized the little box of animal crackers. She was laughing, and she ripped the box open with glee. She put a cracker in her mouth. I was looking over my shoulder and I saw her wave at us, but Grandfather did not look back. He never looked at them.

The woman said something. I started to stop, to look back at her, but Grandfather began moving as fast as he could, as if he was afraid we were being chased by something. When we were out of sight, he slowed to a walk, limping painfully. I looked up at him and saw that there was a smile on his face.

"Did you spend all of our money on food for them?" I asked.

"All of it!" he said. "Do you think your mother will be very angry with me? I hope I am not in big, big trouble with her."

"I don't understand you," I said. "Why did you do it?"

"Because I dream a better world. A world in which no child goes to bed hungry. That is Indian land, that is the world I dream and see."

"But that's just a dream and we . . ."

"Dreams are everything!" he said. Then he almost fell. His face was white with pain. I began to wonder if he would make it all the way home.

"What you just did wasn't a dream," I said.

"No. When your mother gets home and finds out, it will seem more like a nightmare. She will say I have brought too much of the innocence of the pueblo into our house. Perhaps she will be so angry she will spit bullets at me."

We walked on in silence for a while. As we got closer to home, Grandfather stopped to rest against the side of a building.

"I still don't know why you did it."

"Because you can only save the world one day at a time. Because that is what men with dreams do. And mostly because I will remember the look in their eyes as long as I live," said Grandfather, "and it will make me feel good when times are bad."

"But you never looked at her. How could you have seen . . ."

Then I stopped because I knew. He would see it in his dreams, in the world he shaped with his hands.

We walked again and I began to think about my Grandfather and the world he saw. Maybe that promise everybody wanted me to keep wasn't so bad after all. Maybe Grandfather was showing me how the promise could be kept.

Just one day at a time. Dream and do one day's

work to make it true and a promise as big as forever didn't seem so long.

We were almost home. I was curious about something.

"How come we brought back the empty sacks?"

"Your mother saves them. I thought if I at least brought those back she might be less angry." He seemed gloomy about what she would say. "Do you think it will help?"

"No," I said, and laughed.

I knew she would be angry at first, but soon she would understand, perhaps because of the look in a small girl's eyes she would see in her dreams.

As we started up the driveway, Grandfather was in so much pain he had to lean on me just to walk.

"What will we do without food?" I asked.

"Be hungry for a while," said Grandfather.

"How are you going to explain this to Mother?"

Grandfather sighed as I opened the back door for him.

"I was hoping you would explain it," he said.

"You're on your own," I said.

Chapter ❧ Twenty-one

The next morning the world seemed different.

Mother still hadn't found a job. Grandfather's legs were swollen, and we had to carry him into the kitchen for breakfast.

"I am glad you are not angry," said Grandfather.

"I might as well be angry at the sun for being yellow and high in the sky. We are who we are. I am sad about it but I am proud, too," said Mother. She patted her stomach. "Besides, I need to lose some weight anyway."

She had her best dress on, and she was smiling as she went out the door.

"Good luck finding a job!" Grandfather shouted after her.

She waved from inside the car as she let it idle for a while so the engine could warm up.

"Now there goes a brave woman," said Grandfather. "She's facing the day with a smile and she hasn't even had one cup of coffee! That's what I call real courage."

There was nothing in the house to make a meal of, but Grandfather insisted on being in the kitchen for breakfast anyway. I sat next to him.

"Do I still have ears?" asked Grandfather. "I think your mother almost chewed them off last night."

"She was really mad at you." It was kind of nice to see somebody else get into trouble instead of me.

"Just at first. But then she knew a little girl slept last night with a full belly and a smile in her heart, and there was no anger in her."

"I think I am very hungry, Grandfather," I said. I heard the car back out of the driveway and I knew Mother was gone.

"I know where she is, don't you?"

I started to speak, but he interrupted.

"No, close your eyes. Then you can see her as I see her. Where is she now?"

I shrugged.

"I shape the world in my hands," said Grandfather, holding his hand out with the palms up, as if he carried something heavy. "We are on Indian land and your mother is here with me. Do you know where she is?"

Now I understood.

"By the stove, cooking frybread!" I said, keeping

my eyes shut tight. Though I couldn't see him, I knew Grandfather was smiling.

We had so much fun dreaming up breakfast that we dreamed up lunch, too. That was so great we almost started on dinner, but Grandfather said we better not get too greedy. We should save something for later.

I was still hungry, but it didn't bother me so much. Somehow my grandfather and I got through the rest of the day.

Mother came home tired but excited. It wasn't a sure thing, but she thought she had a chance at a job. They might even call her first thing tomorrow morning. But even if they didn't give her the job, she was sure she could find one somewhere.

"We won't starve," said Mother. "A woman at the employment agency told me that as long as I have a house and a stove, we can get food stamps to buy groceries with until I find a job. I don't know where to go get them but I'll look into that tomorrow when I am looking for work. Whatever happens, we'll make out somehow."

We all went to bed hungry, but in a world shaped by my grandfather's hands.

I thought I would be too hungry to sleep. Instead I felt more at ease than I could ever remember, even though I lived in the city, we were poor, and the world was sometimes a terrible place.

I missed my father, but he was not gone. His dreams would live again in me. And that was a good thing.

My father once said something that seemed sad then and sadder now. It was about traveling and about life.

He said there was no loneliness like having miles to go and promises to keep. I didn't understand it back then but now I thought I did. All the bad things were still there, still waiting for me in the miles ahead. But tonight, none of those things seemed to matter. Good things were waiting out there, too.

Tonight, I would imagine that the blankets were Grandfather's hands and I would pull them up over me.

Tonight I would sleep in the world in Grandfather's hands.

About the Author

"When you know too much about life as Indians live it, the sadness is somehow always there," says Craig Strete. But there is still what he calls "the heart and soul" of *The World in Grandfather's Hands:* "hope which gives courage to look at the night and see things. And the power of dreams which brings day from night."

Born in Fort Wayne, Indiana, to a Cherokee father and a white mother, Craig Kee Strete earned his B.A. in theater arts at Wright State University and his M.F.A. in creative writing at the University of California at Irvine. He is the author of several novels, short-story collections, and picture books for children, as well as novels, stories, and plays for adults. *The World in Grandfather's Hands* is his first book for Clarion. Mr. Strete lives alternately in Idaho, California, and Europe.